MRS SMITH'S SUSPECTS
CARRIE, GARY, BEL, & HARRY

JINNY ALEXANDER

ISBN Paperback: 978-1-916814-12-7

ISBN Large Print Paperback: 978-1-916814-14-1

ISBN ebook: 978-1-916814-13-4

ISBN audiobook: 978-1-916814-15-8

Cover Design: Wicked Good Book Covers (www.wickedgoodbookcovers.com)
Cover and title page artwork: aileemarieart (www.instagram.com/aileemarie_art)
High Street Drawing of Little Wittering: Jinny Alexander
Photo of Amber: Jinny's parents' wedding photos

Visit www.jinnyalexander.com

Dedication

The Mrs Smith's Suspects series is in memory of my
grandmother:
Jean Alexander (29th July 1921 – 10th October 1979),
and her guide dog, Amber.

This book is also dedicated to my wonderful Uncle Graham:
"Our lives are full of memories of our lovely Uncle Graham.
That doesn't make it easier to find a way to say 'em."

AMBER 1970

Thank you also to Emily Trapp, who suggested the name
'Amity' for Mrs Smith's guide dog. It's the perfect name!

A note to my American-English readers

I'm so glad you're here! I'm a British author, living in the Republic of Ireland, and all my books are set in Ireland or the UK. As such, I use British English in my writing so you'll notice a few extra letters – Us after Os, for instance, and Ls that come in pairs. I make up for these extras by using fewer Zs...

I hope you'll enjoy my natural English voice and immerse yourselves fully into my UK and Irish settings and characters, but if you're still not convinced, I recommend a nice cup of tea.

Over here, a nice cup of tea fixes almost everything.

Love, Jinny xx

Special mention

Some time ago, I ran a contest through my newsletter for a cameo mention in a book. The lucky winner, **MaryEllen**, nominated her daughter, **April**, to be named, and sent me so much interesting information I could have written a whole book about them! You'll find April visiting Little Wittering, where she gets caught up in the events as they unfold.

Little Wittering High Street

Original sketch by Jinny Alexander ©2025

Chapter One

By the time a competent member of the police force arrived in the Little Wittering library, I was almost certain I had deduced the identity of Charlotte's killer.

Amity nudged my leg with her cold, wet nose and I bent to rub her silky head. "Not long now, I shouldn't think," I reassured her, although I supposed she thought she was the one doing the reassuring, now I think about it. She's trained to be reassuring and I'm sure she realised something was amiss, as she usually just lies under the table in the library's meeting room and snores softly while Phyllis and I join in with the chatter about whatever book we happen to be reading in Book Club that week.

On that particular Tuesday, we had been discussing one of Dennis's favourite Agatha Christie books – Dennis is my husband – and I must say it's most unusual for us to 'do' a book he enjoys. We'd been chatting about it over our breakfast that morning – Dennis and I, that is, not the ladies from the book club – and he doesn't often have anything much to say over breakfast, so that was a pleasant deviation from our norm and it goes to show that even when one is in their seventies, there is still a chance of something new.

Dennis usually reads the newspaper while I listen to the radio and think about the day ahead, and every now and then he'll read something aloud if he finds it particularly interesting or thinks I might like to hear about it. There hadn't been anything of interest though, as very little happens in Little Wittering, and I wasn't paying any attention to the radio at all as I was thinking about the book, and I said as much to Dennis when he offered to pour me another cup of tea.

"What's that, dear?" I'd said, but you mustn't think I'm going at all deaf as my hearing is terribly good. Of course, he knows that, so he guessed at once that my mind was elsewhere and he asked me what it was I was thinking about and that's where it started.

"Just getting my mind ready for book club," I said, and he said, "Oh, yes, Sal, that's today." I don't know why he never seems to remember, because I've been going along to the library for the book club every Tuesday morning for the last goodness knows, so it really shouldn't be any kind of surprise to him by now. I would probably have given him one of those withering kind of glares, but my ability to glare effectively vanished with my eyesight so I just tutted.

He said what was I tutting about when he was the one offering to pour tea so it must be a good book if it had me so distracted. He had a point, as it is quite a good book, and when I told him, he got a bit cross and said he'd have listened to it with me if only I'd told him. I must say I thought that a bit rich. I've been listening to it from the garden chairs while he's been pottering about at the roses and whatnot, and he could quite easily have heard it if only he'd been paying attention.

There followed a most animated discussion about the murders and the killer and the method and it was a terribly exciting change for us, and then it was nine and Harriet was at the door and that was that. Harriet is the carer, and although I'm sure we could do without, she is awfully sweet and does some useful things like checking we have all the groceries we need and making sure things are in date. Dennis could do that quite easily but Harriet hasn't fully trusted him after the incident with the microwave, although I don't see the connection, myself.

"Morning Mrs Smith," she'd trilled in that cheerful way she has, and she bustled herself down the small hallway and into the kitchen before I'd even got as far as the kitchen doorway. She lets herself in, most days, which I suppose is good practice for the terribly infirm as one never knows whether they are able to manage. However, Dennis and I are still quite agile, as we are only in our seventies and not at all decrepit, and I may not be able to see anything much but I do know the way to my own front door, a tipple of wine on a Friday evening notwithstanding.

Harriet and Dennis had their habitual debate about which of them would partake of which chores and whether one of them would bring me to the library. Dennis hadn't said, but I had the feeling it was a pleasant enough day, so I inquired of Harriet as to the weather and she agreed it was perfectly mild and not a cloud to be seen. With this proclamation, my mind was made up and I said quite firmly that I would walk with Amity and arrange to collect Phyllis on my way, and that settled the matter and they bickered about something else instead until I suggested Harriet may like to first find Phyl's telephone number to save me the trouble, and then help me with my hair, to which she readily agreed. After I made the arrangements with Phyl, Harriet and I left Dennis grumbling in the kitchen about the crossword and set off to the bedroom where she could attend to my hair.

Not an hour later, having met Phyllis on the corner, and her having slipped her arm through mine while we let Amity have a little run in the green space at the corner before reattaching her harness, we had trundled into Little Wittering Library, settled ourselves in the back room with the ladies from the book club, and were midway through our second cup of tea and the murder of poor Betty Barnard from Bexhill, when there was an awful kerfuffle from the main part of the building and even Amity gave a little bark of concern.

A moment after the noise, Carrie's voice carried through to the meeting room in a terribly shrill tone, saying somebody needed medical attention and was anyone in the library any kind of medic, or should she call for an ambulance.

Of course, Ashwini jumped up, or as much as one can jump to one's feet when one is fifty-eight, but she is far nimbler than Phyllis or me so I expect she moved quickly enough, given the circumstances. Ashwini said to someone that she wasn't a doctor by any means but when one has been married to Dr Patil for so long as she, one does pick up some useful skills. She's also borne five children so that goes a long way, wouldn't you agree? She had to manoeuvre around Joan, as she had been sitting opposite me, with her back to the window, and Barbara, Josephine, and Mary all on her other side, so I expect she was quite hemmed in, but once she'd got herself past Joan's walking frame without any incident, she beetled past me in such a rush as to cause a breeze around my arms and to alert Amity to her feet – she hadn't bothered to get up with the bark, as she must have sensed that whatever the kerfuffle, it wasn't placing me or her in any danger. I patted her head gently and she soon returned to her station beneath the table but I wouldn't be at all surprised if she'd kept one ear cocked, just in case. Once Ashwini had departed from our group, there was at first one of those strange silences that tends to fall when a group of people is given some unsuspecting news, and then after a moment or two, everyone began chattering all at once and making assumptions about the situation, and everyone got carried away and I quite lost track of the conversation in the hubbub.

"Phyl," I said to my dear friend, "what on earth is going on?"

"Someone has been taken ill," Phyl whispered in a most excitable tone. "Someone has found someone collapsed in the cookery section or somewhere. Ashwini has gone to see if she can help. Goodness!" At that, Phyl fell silent again save for some quite audible gulps of her rapidly-cooling tea.

Into her silence, the other ladies of our little book club offered their speculations and observations on the matter.

"Who is it?" Joan asked in her shaky voice.

"No, no idea ... can't possibly tell ..." someone else said.

"... behind the bookshelves ..."

"... in the non-fic, I think ..."

"... doctor coming?" From the direction of the voice, I presumed that to have been from Mary, and next to her, at the end of the table, Isobel added, "She probably had a fit... I saw someone have a fit, once, when I was in the Spar with Mum."

"Is it the heat? That could cause anyone to faint..."

And so it went in a rush of speculation and supposition and it was all I could do to make out who it was who spoke each conjecture, because just as soon as I distinguished one voice, so another cut over and I was lost again. After some minutes during which I became increasingly baffled, I held up my hand much as I would have done in my teaching days when I needed to bring an enthusiastic class of teenagers to order. "One at a time, please. I simply can't make head nor tail of it if you all talk at once, as you very well know."

The ladies fell obediently silent, and I imagined them to be regaining their composure and gathering their wits, as it were. My hearing is terribly sharp, but when several people talk at once and in great excitement, there is only so much one can be expected to follow. They are usually most understanding of my limitations and have learned over the years how best to address the group in order that I may keep up with the communications just as adeptly as they, but one can be forgiven, I suppose, for lapses in the wake of an exciting or dramatic event such as the discovery of a real-live body in the midst of our genteel discussions about a fictional one.

Of course, I am getting ahead of myself, as at that moment, most of us present couldn't possibly have known poor Charlotte was actually *dead*.

As a point of fact, we didn't even know it was *Charlotte*.

After another moment where Mary and Josephine and Barbara all began at once, Phyllis, who used to be a librarian so is used to sorting things out, spoke up and said, "All right then, Mary first, then Barbara, then you, Josephine, and we'll see if that covers things well enough for Sally," for which I was most grateful and reminded once again of why Phyllis and I are such dear friends. She has adapted to my loss of vision almost as well as have I, if not equally well, and I really can't say what I would have done without her. We have been friends for over fifty years, and through just as much thick and thin as if we were married to each other and not to Dennis and Frederick, so that will tell you how close we are to one another.

"I can see through to the main room from here," Mary said, which was helpful, if a little unnecessary. As I had my back to the main room, and Mary sat on the opposite side of the wide table about which we gathered, it went without saying that she faced into the larger room of the library, where all the books are housed. She was seated at the furthest end of that side of the table, so I deduced that she would be able to see a good deal further into the library than anyone else at the table, and I expect she might be able to see the desk quite well, as the layout of the library has not changed very much in the last twenty years.

There is a bright walkway between the desk and the two meeting rooms, with a handy skylight above to let the light into the room. It must be said, despite the lack of imagination in the overall shape and design, the skylights were a welcome aberration to the rest of it, so the architect must have had some sense of ambition despite the limitations of the seventies planning department. Overall, the library is a bright building, which I find most useful as the dark shadowy shapes of the bookshelves have greater contrast to the light patches, and combined with my memories of the place and Amity's clever guidance, it is not at all complicated for me to get around when I need to. As there is no dividing door between the meeting rooms and the main area, merely one of those clever corrugated sliding contraptions with which it is possible to afford some privacy, and the windows are those big metal-framed types one would find terribly ugly if one were able to see them, the meeting rooms also have a welcome brightness about them. They can become fusty in damp weather, but as it was a bright May morning that was of no matter to the events at all.

When the book club meets, it is not customary to close the divider, as it is felt amongst the library staff that visitors are encouraged by the ability to see the library being used for a multitude of purposes and that it fosters an air of community spirit.

Whilst I appreciate the intentions, I am *on the fence* as it were, as to how I feel about this. Were the room contained and closed off, I would find it considerably easier to follow the conversations without the distractions of the main library to contend with, but then I may lose some awareness as to the goings-on beyond this meeting space, although to be perfectly honest about it, the divider is of little use in terms of muffling the sound. Of course, as one might very well imagine, there is not much noise emitting from a library most of the time, so it is only terribly distracting when there are young children in the vicinity. As is only sensible, as a general rule, they do try to restrict children's activities to certain times of the day that do not interfere with such events as the regular Tuesday morning book club or the Wednesday morning craft activities or the Women's Institute meetings that occur every last Thursday. As you might guess, the events for adult participants tend to take place in the mornings and evenings, leaving the afternoons free for children's activities and suchlike. There are some amongst the group who are inclined to argue that the morning times do impose a certain amount of restriction as to who may attend, and Josephine gets terribly cross about book club as she is only able to attend in school holidays due to her commitments in the primary school, but I suppose one simply can't cater for everyone, no matter the intentions.

"Salamander Smith," Phyllis hissed loudly and impolitely from my righthand side, reminding me immediately of our time in teaching college when we were bright young things of about seventeen, although of course I hadn't ever been referred to as Salamander Smith until some years later, once I became married to Dennis. "Are you even listening?"

I am not the type to blush, but I do know when I am in the wrong and as such, I am perfectly gracious in accepting a little telling-off if it is deserved. As such, I apologised immediately for having allowed my mind to drift and we all had a little chuckle about that. The drifting of minds is the topic of many of our conversations, and only to be expected by the time one has reached the age of retirement, which describes at least half of us in the book club, by now, although not so many of us older ladies were there that day for one reason or another. Joan is our eldest, and she is eighty-seven. She has one of those walking-frame contraptions that takes up a great deal of space, which is why we try to put her at the end of the table. She can be a bit doddery at times, but her mind is terribly sharp. Josephine is a little younger than Phyl and I, although we are quite good friends, and then at the other end of the scale, as it were, there is Mary, who is about twenty or thereabouts, and a lovely little thing, and Isobel, who is quite new. Both are students at the county university, who come along because they happen to have Tuesday mornings off and enjoy discussing the books. I presume Isobel to also be around twenty, as she is in her second year, but I can't be certain.

Phyllis, as you know, is my dear friend, and she sat beside me that morning, just as she usually does. To her other side, sat Kimberly, who must be around thirty, as she was amongst the final cohort of my days overseeing 5S in St Cuthbert's Secondary School. I recall her as a quiet, determined little thing, although she has developed some confidence in more recent years. She has children in the primary school, so she settled quite quickly into becoming a bit of a homebird, which was a surprise as she was quite the academic, although despite being a diligent student, if I recall, her results rarely reflected her efforts. From time to time, she mutters half-heartedly about looking for a job, but it can be terribly difficult for a woman to place herself back into the workforce after such a break, especially once one factors in after-school childcare and suchlike, as she does like to remind us. If you ask me, I don't believe she is terribly fussed about the notion of a job, but nonetheless, she is terribly practical and I am fond of her.

Phyl dug me in the ankle with the toe of her shoe.

"Sorry," I said again, turning my face attentively towards Mary's voice at the diagonally opposite place at the table to that at which I sat. "Would you mind repeating your observations?"

It seemed she'd been the first amongst us to be alerted to the commotion in the library by the unusual sight of a swift movement in the main room, and I must say I was terribly impressed at her observational skills until I considered how little attention she must have been paying to our book club conversation if she were distracted by a movement amongst the bookshelves. I said as much to her in a most jovial manner and everyone had another little chuckle before we remembered the sorry fact that beyond the bookshelves there lay a person apparently in need of medical assistance, awaiting the attention of a doctor or ambulance of whosoever arrived first upon the scene.

Chapter Two

After some time had passed – perhaps as much as ten minutes, although we had some debate about that – Ashwini had not returned and there were some sounds of quiet commotion emitting from the main room, so Kimberly said perhaps one of us ought to go and see if there was anything to be done and the others of us readily agreed. Aside from the immediate dilemma as to whether we should proceed with our conversations about *The ABC Murders* without Ashwini, there was a unanimous agreement that we would very much like to know what was happening amongst the bookshelves, in case it was anything exciting or dreadful.

"Or both," said Barbara, from across the table. She can be terribly dry in her manner and one can quite imagine her at one of those open-microphone literary events one hears about in the Grape and Hop now and again. The Grape and Hop is the more upmarket of the High Street pubs, although Dennis and I much prefer the hotel, which has a delightfully comfortable lounge and a tendency towards live piano music at the weekends. The high street's other pub, The Leaky Tap, is far too complicated for me to negotiate these days, with its higgledy-piggledy interior and stench of stale beer and cigarettes. One is no longer permitted to smoke cigarettes inside any such public building, of course, but the smell seems to have lingered in that particular establishment. One tries not to imagine what other unsavoury detritus may be welded to the floor by the unwashed spills of beer, which reminded me at once of the matter in hand.

"We don't mind a bit of dreadful, do we ladies?" Barbara said. There was a gentle waft of air and that funny glugging sound of a book being fanned, so I guessed at once that Barbara was making another of her funny little jokes about our current murder mystery, and joined in the laughter.

"Or exciting," I said, adding a firm nod of my head to emphasise my agreement on the matter. "Nonetheless, it would be reassuring to know that there is nothing untoward going on."

"Or if anyone needs to offer further assistance," Josephine added. She speaks in a very distinct Liverpudlian accent, so it is easy for me to discern her voice, however lively our conversations may get. When everyone is calm and one takes one's turn in an orderly and sensible manner, I cope terribly well. Most of the ladies have quite distinct voices, which is an enormous help to me, as I'm sure you can imagine. Ashwini is from India, although they have been here for at least thirty years, I should think; all the children attended the local schools and are quite grown up by now. She has a tendency to speak in that rather fast way that is typical of so many Indians who speak English as their second language. It really is marvellous, albeit a little complicated to follow if one isn't giving one's full attention to the matter. Dr Patil is Ashwini's husband and although he has the most wonderful bedside manner, he does speak terribly quickly. We had a little joke about it once, after I misunderstood some instruction or the other and had an unnecessary extraction of blood. It is, he explained, a way in which his compatriots prove to one another their competency in the language. "That is all well and good," I had retorted, "but if one speaks the most wonderfully grammatical English at such a rate that one cannot be understood, there seems to be little benefit, don't you think?"

Phyl's sing-song Irish lilt is a delight on one's ears, although, of course, Phyllis and I have been dear friends for such a very long time that I would know her voice anywhere. I also find it quite easy to know *when* Joan is speaking during our book club coffee mornings, although it can be terribly difficult to hear what it is she wishes to say. She is terribly sharp, but her voice is as fragile as her body, and when she speaks, we must all fall quiet and give her our utmost attention, which is a courtesy one should afford to any speaker, now I come to think about it.

The others, I'm afraid, are less distinct when everyone speaks at once, although Barbara is one of those people who is terribly dry and witty and if one hasn't got to know her at all well, she is the type who may cause offence at the drop of a hat.

Isobel is a little plummy, while Kimberly and Mary are still quite girlish in their tone, which one may expect from Mary, who is barely out of her childhood, but not at all from Kimberly who was rather reserved and blotchy as a teenager during my later years at St Cuthbert's. As she is now thirty or thereabouts, I expect she has grown out of the blotches, but one hardly likes to ask. We also usually have Gail and Nora, and

Laura from the florist when she can get away, and although we refer to ourselves as 'ladies', Matthew from the vicarage pops along when he can get away, and Old Willie comes with Nora, when he isn't on duty, so we are quite inclusive, as far as it goes. Kimberly has suggested on several occasions that we recruit some more "fit young men," and Joan and Nora get quite on board with the idea of that, despite Willie's protests. Nonetheless, it's not to be, as the men really don't seem inclined to sit around discussing literature on a Tuesday morning, and on this particular day, many of the regulars had made their apologies and we were just the nine of us.

"We could have done with our nurses," Barbara said. "They never come when you come, Josephine. I expect it's you keeps them away."

"Or that it's Whitsun week and they are on holiday." Josephine is quite used to Barbara's teasing, and they are good friends although one would be forgiven for thinking otherwise. I know Josephine quite well enough to imagine her to be poking her tongue out at Barbara in a perfectly childish manner. Of course, Nora has been retired for quite some time, and Gail works in the dentist's surgery, which isn't quite the same thing, but I didn't bother to say so as everyone knows each other well enough by now, so I said, "It's a good job Ashwini is with us, as a doctor's wife is better than nothing," and that brought us right back to wondering where she'd got to.

"Okay, I'll go and find her." As Kimberly was seated beside Phyl, and thus seated on the side of the table with our backs to the open doorway into the main library, it was quite sensible that she be the one to offer to go, so none of us thought anything of it, and it was quickly agreed upon without dissent. There was the rub of a chair on the coarse library carpet, and the soft scent of Kimberly's rose perfume as she left the room. I suspect it's one of those cheaper ones from Boots, rather than an expensive designer type, as it is inclined to make Phyl's nose tickle, but I can't be sure.

I decided that I may as well take the opportunity to pop along to the lavatories, even though I had been before we started our meeting, as I always do. I said as much to Phyllis, and she said she'd come along too, and Isobel said she'd hang onto Amity for me if I didn't need her.

"Sure, won't we manage well enough," Phyl agreed, so I gave Amity the instruction to remain just where she was, and said to Isobel that she would probably just snooze under the table and hardly notice at all. "Tell her to 'Wait' in a nice firm tone if she gets up at all, and you'll find she is perfectly obedient about it," I said, and off we went.

The lavatories in the library are just outside the meeting room, so I didn't imagine we would find out anything useful. Besides, as I think I mentioned, at that point in the proceedings, we didn't know that anyone was dead, yet alone poor Charlotte, so we didn't think too much about doing any kind of sleuthing but only about the pressing of a cup of tea upon our bladders.

I took up my cane, tucked my hand into Phyl's arm, and she led me off, and it was only as we came out of the lavatories again that we heard Ashwini's voice suggesting very calmly that she really didn't think there was anything she could do. She added something about not being very optimistic about the paramedics either, which caused me to prick up my ears and hesitate in my steps, I can tell you.

Beside me, Phyl, too, stopped walking, and we stood frozen in position like two children playing Grandmother's footsteps. I gave her arm a little squeeze to warn her not to make a noise, and of course, she understood immediately and didn't utter a peep. There was still the chatter coming from the Book Club ladies, which made it difficult to hear anything much else, so in one of those moments of perfect synchronicity that Phyl and I are partial to, we edged our way a little further from the Book Club room and a little nearer to the location from which Ashwini's voice had carried.

The layout of the library is quite simple as it is one of those single-story unimaginative buildings from the 1970s. Although the interior has been updated once or twice over the years, one supposes there is very little one can do for the shape of the place within the limited remit of a council budget. As one enters the library, one comes through a functional rectangular lobby. In the lobby, there is a wide main door onto the pathway, and two internal doors opposite the outer door; one for entry and one through which to exit. They are side by side on the longer side of the lobby, which one might imagine to have been the original exterior wall before some vote-collecting council official declared it a good idea to allocate money for the porch to be added. The twin doors are divided by a stretch of the wall approximately the same width as each of the doors, and the last time I was able to see the front of the library, it boasted an assortment of those large solid letters one sticks to government buildings. One supposes they were designed to spell out the name of Little Wittering

Library but somehow managed to say **Litt e Witt ring Libra y** instead. One must wonder where the letters go, when they fall off, and why it is that no one seems to manage to replace them. Of course, that was a good fifteen years ago, so they may have been updated, but no one has ever said "Sally, you wouldn't believe it, but the front of the library has had an update," so I can only imagine it has yet to occur. I haven't thought to ask whether more of the confounded lettering has succumbed to the abyss, so I suppose it could say **itt it ib** by now, for all I know.

Once one enters, through the left-hand door as one approaches, there is a long desk to one's right. This desk is so arranged that one must pass it on the way in and also on the way out. Those stationed thereat may look across the whole of the library with not a great deal of effort, which one must presume was the intention of the setup. Of course, the copious amount of shelving must hinder one's view to some extent, and I imagine a librarian must need to utilise the full sense of their hearing in order to remain vigilant. Phyllis will back me up on this as she was an excellent librarian once she gave up on her teaching career to find something altogether quieter.

To the left of the entry door is the children's section, although you will not be at all surprised to hear that this is not an area I spend any time in. The children's area used to be a bright and cheerful area, adorned with colourful posters of book characters; large beanbags, and the kind of tables and chairs one finds in a modern primary school reception classroom. Books were arranged in low, easy-to-access boxes, for the little ones, and in the expected neatly-alphabetised shelves for older readers. I don't believe it has changed very much over the years, and it tends to smell very faintly of either urine or bleach, depending on the day.

The entire building is largely symmetrical, and on the opposite side of the desk from the children's area, there is a section designated for computers and other technological contraptions such as a rather cumbersome photocopier. There is a most distinct smell from a photocopier and I must confess it is a smell of which I am rather fond. It reminds me of moments of blissful interlude away from a particularly challenging class of third-years, during what seemed to be an interminably long autumn term, in which I found just as many reasons to nip along to photocopy worksheets as I possibly could. Fortunately, I moved away from that school shortly thereafter, to take up a position in St Cuthbert's, where I remained for the rest of my teaching career. When one has been a teacher for as long as I, there are certain scents that one associates with pleasant reminisces, such as chalk dust after a productive and lively discussion on the merits of *Othello*, or altogether less enjoyable memories such as unwashed PE kits stuffed inside duffle bags on a Wednesday afternoon.

I'm afraid I do seem to have digressed somewhat, but the rest of the main room in the library is taken up with the majority of the adult reading, as one might expect. Fiction is to the centre and left, and non-fiction is arranged to the right, beside the computers.

Two meeting rooms adjoin the main room, at the back of the building, and it is within one of these that the Tuesday-morning book club adjourns. One may be forgiven for presuming there is little to discern between the two meeting rooms, but Phyllis and I are in perfect agreement that we much prefer the one to the left as one approaches. The two rooms are of similar size, shape, and furnishings, and indeed, a minority of the ladies have expressed preference for the right-hand room, largely due to the fact it holds the tea-making facilities. It is also fractionally further from the children's section, which you will agree has some merit. Those in favour of the left room voice such advantages as proximity to the lavatories, but the main advantage is that in the right-hand room, the window has become jammed shut, whilst the left-hand room window has not.

On the particular Tuesday in question, the weather was most clement, as is only too fitting for the Whitsun week. Even though it was a half-term holiday, the schoolchildren must have been enjoying the park or some other outdoor activity, and the library was blissfully quiet but rather warm. Thus, we had gravitated without question towards the left-hand room and someone had thrown open the window and we were all enjoying the gentle breeze. Of course, Josephine had needed to close it temporarily for the window cleaners, but reopened it just as soon as they had finished our window and passed on to the next set. Without such relief of the open window, the room was inclined to become stuffy and hot, with a prevailing whiff of body odour in summer.

Of course, Phyllis and I were not in either of the meeting rooms, as at the moment which I describe, we were in the main library room, inching towards Ashwini's voice, step by stealthy step. Together, we shuffled silently around the first of the enormous bookshelves, which used to house **A-E** if my memory serves me well, although I wouldn't be at all surprised if that had changed. I clutched Phyl's arm, and kept my ears pricked as we edged closer to the central stacks, tapping my cane as softly as I could on the laminated wooden floor. Towering shadows marked out the bookshelves; the light from the skylights fractionally brightening the aisles to a slightly lighter shade of the fuzzy and indistinct greys that are my only view of the world nowadays.

An assortment of voices drifted from the far side of the room, in the section where, as far as I know, the non-fiction titles are still contained. I have had little need to venture between the shelves in a very long time, as I simply trot up to the desk and have a nice little chat with one of the librarians, and they suggest a nice audio book and organise the borrowing side of things. Whilst at first I preferred to take some level of responsibility for the selection, I have come to accept the delight of being surprised by whatever Carrie suggests, and have discovered some perfectly delectable titles in this manner. Charlotte is very young and hasn't Carrie's experience, so she is less inclined to select something entirely to my taste. Of course, I still give it a listen, and report back, and then we have a little debate about it, and Charlotte tells me she makes a little note of it and adjusts the criteria so she might find a more enjoyable match for the next one, but she has yet to live up to the promise and I much prefer to rely on Carrie's expertise, on the whole. I expect she really does have a little notebook about me, and scribbles detailed comments to keep track of it all, although it might just as well be that she simply plucks whatever it is that comes to hand, but she is more of the type to have a notebook, I should think.

Carrie has been a fixture in Little Wittering library for even longer than that blessed photocopier, so I recognised her voice quite easily amongst the others. Nonetheless, I had only once before heard the shrill edge of worry that it held on this particular Tuesday, and that was some years ago when a particularly mischievous and inadequately-supervised toddler had scaled the **O-Z** shelf in Older Readers and had to be removed by a somewhat precarious venture up the step-ladder. I almost wished I had been able to see the excitement, although I was able to imagine it most vividly as there was quite the commentary from everyone present.

Among the low burble of voices from across the room, Carrie's voice rose still more sharply as she said, "Is there any breath at all?" in a kind of hopeful, desperate way, and Phyl and I froze in horror.

"Goodness," Phyl whispered, "you don't think someone is actually dead?"

"It sounds as if that might be the case," I whispered back. "Can you see anything?"

She stretched away from me; her arm pulling away from me, and I supposed her to be craning her neck to peer around the shelving and towards the voices.

"Tell me what you can see," I whispered.

"Hang on."

I found myself tugged a little towards the main desk, if my sense of direction were accurate, and my cane tapped into the bottom of one of the shelves. I guessed us to be somewhere around the **K-O** section, but we may have still been nearer to the lavatories than that. Besides, I imagine the system to have evolved and adapted as those popular modern authors squeeze out the Austens and the Dickens. Whilst awaiting Phyllis's description of the events, I amused myself for a moment with imagining the shelves waltzing around all over the place, shuffling into new positions as they accommodated new arrivals, much in the manner of the anthropomorphic wardrobes in that animated version of Beauty and the Beast. I must admit that I found that to be an awfully enjoyable movie, even though Dennis insisted I was far too old for it, what with being in my forties when it came out, but he came along to the pictures with me nonetheless and ate more than his share of the popcorn, if my memory is correct about it.

"Well?" I said, when Phyllis still hadn't said anything.

She gave my arm a swift tug towards the floor, so I guessed at once she must be bending to squint beneath the shelves in the hope of a clearer view. "Someone is lying on the floor over in non-fic. Round about Gardening or Cookery, I should think."

Phyllis was the librarian-in-charge here in Little Wittering for a number of years, overlapping with Carrie for a year or so before she gave it all up, so I expect she was fairly accurate about the location, although as I already mentioned, I suppose things have been rearranged a little since then.

"There's a bit of a huddle, but I can see their legs."

"Whose legs?"

"Well now, sure aren't there lots of legs, under the shelves, but only one set appears to be lying down. Hang on."

She tugged me upwards again and dragged me along a fraction more, not even bothering to be quiet about it, and I did wish that I was able to take a look myself as although Phyl is usually terribly good about telling me things in a sensible kind of a way, she really wasn't up to her usual standard at that precise moment. From the pull of her arm on mine, I guessed she must be bending down again in an attempt to peer under the shelving to see if that mightn't give her a better look at things from that angle. I released her arm from mine, in order to prevent her toppling us both to the ground, and stood there with my hand on the shelf to anchor me.

"Well?"

"Sensible shoes that probably belong to Carrie, those smart black –"

"It can't be Carrie; I can hear her speaking."

"Not the lying-down legs, you daft old bat. I can't see those again now. Everyone's moved. Carrie is standing behind the bookshelves."

I patted the air around me until I found Phyllis again, and dug my fingers into her waist. "Phyllis, will you just remember who it is you are talking to and describe things in a sensible and coherent way, for goodness sake?"

She gave one of her little huffs. "I can see a large and slightly-sagging bookshelf, probably Hobbies and Interests, as that's the longest one in that section, and if I had to make a wild guess, I'd say it's closer to the Gardening end of things, which means if the angle is as I think it is, the head might be in Cooking, and there are, hang on ... three, four pairs of legs – the upright kind, that is – and one pair on the floor – ouch!"

"I would imagine even that idiotic Doofus Finbury would be able to tell you that if a person is standing in a library, their legs are most likely to be on the floor, were he present. I presume you mean that three or four people are standing, and one unfortunate person is not?" That gave me a little shiver of unpleasantness and I added that I supposed someone may indeed telephone the police and the idiot child now known as Police Constable Finbury would arrive like a bad smell of drains on a hot day.

She nudged me back, with far more sharpness than I had exercised in my prodding of her, but I was still imagining the unwelcome arrival of Doofus Finbury, so didn't rise to it, and she went on. "One set must belong to Ashwini. The small, delicate black court shoes, I should think. One pair is Carrie's, like I told you. Men's laced up work boots, and a pair of trainers with jeans that could belong to anyone I should think."

"Look around the rest of the library. What else can you see?"

"Bo – oof!"

"Phyllis! If you dare to say books, I will prod you in the eye with my cane."

With that, Phyl led me onwards, with more determination and a good deal less of the covert tiptoeing and ducking under bookshelves. I deduced we were progressing towards the desk, which I ascertained not only from the direction in which Phyllis led me, but also from the soft *swsh-swsh* that the exit door tends to make in a breeze. It has not closed properly since about 2003, unless it is locked, as they tend to do in the winter but don't bother with when the day is pleasant and warm. Besides the noise of the door, there was also a quiet, regular bleep, as one may expect when a printer or photocopying machine is demanding one's attention, and as we neared the desk, the library telephone began to ring, which only served to reinforce my certainty that we were mere feet from the counter.

"Oh bother it," came Carrie's voice from further away. "You can wait."

I supposed she was talking to the telephone in that way one sometimes addresses inanimate objects in times of stress, so it seemed reasonable to presume she was not intending to answer the call. In all my time in Little Wittering, I have not known Carrie to let the library phone go unanswered during her times of duty.

"Goodness," I said to Phyl, under my breath, "It must be something serious."

Chapter Three

Phyl and I returned to the meeting room, in which sat the remainder of our book club ladies. Amity rose to her feet to greet me with a wet nose pushed against my hand, and I gave her ears a little fondle. When I had got myself seated, she sat against my feet, which is always terribly comforting. She is a dear to know how reassuring it can be to know she is attentive and close, and I gave her another little rub about her ears as she does enjoy that.

As it turned out, while Phyl and I had been in the lavatories, or perhaps whilst we loitered amongst the shelving during our unsuccessful attempt to find out what might be going on, Kimberly had returned from her own investigative mission. I suspect she must have returned whilst we were using the facilities, otherwise I am quite certain we would have heard her passing us by, or Phyllis would have mentioned it. Once Phyllis and I had got ourselves comfortable, Kimberly and Phyl took turns to tell the rest of us what they had learned about the situation.

"Charlotte," Kimberly announced in a tone that managed to impart both the solemnity of the occasion and a great deal of dramatic impact, "seems to be dead."

There was a gasp around the table, and one of the ladies said, "Goodness," and Barbara said something altogether more colourful. I must say I entirely agreed with the sentiment, as it was quite the shock and one does not expect a person's demise during a regular Tuesday Book Club meeting, even if the topic of discussion *is* an Agatha Christie murder mystery.

Joan said, "What's that Barbara?" but I expect it from disbelief or shock or some such feeling as there is nothing wrong with her hearing.

"Charlotte," Kimberly said again, "is dead."

Charlotte, I should explain, is another of the Little Wittering librarians. She is terribly young and I wouldn't think she is out of her twenties, judging by her manner and lack of professionalism. Nonetheless, she is at least vaguely competent and can be perfectly pleasant when she puts her mind to it, and had been brought in to replace Dafydd as he prepared for his transfer to the larger library in Chattering. Charlotte hadn't been with us long at all; she had only arrived in Little Wittering Library about six months ago, to be trained into the role. Dafydd was terribly helpful and well-suited to the role of head librarian, and I had been sorry to lose him. As one may imagine, Charlotte's promotion caused quite the upset, and almost led to Carrie's early retirement, but they seemed to have sorted it out, and everything had been ticking along quite nicely as far as I was able to observe from popping in once a week.

"What happened?" Mary asked the question which I imagined to be on many of our tongues.

"Do they *know*?" Isobel's voice was high and worried. For a minute or so, there was another kerfuffle of speculation, although how anyone might have an answer of any accuracy seemed altogether impossible at that point in the proceedings.

"She was too young for it to have been a stroke," Josephine said, and Barbara said in that dry tone of hers that strokes could happen to any of us at any time and young people had aneurysms all the time. Phyl said it was hardly *all* the time, and off they all went again arguing it out.

It was as I sat and listened that I began to put a few snippets of information together in my head, and a terrible thought came to me. Before I could think of keeping it to myself I said, "Can we be quite sure it wasn't deliberate?"

There was a bit of a silence, so I imagine my words had been quite the shock, but you can be assured that I had a perfectly good reason for this conjecture, and had not simply plucked it from the air without due course, even if I hadn't quite intended to say it out loud.

"You mean she did it herself?" Kimberly said, and one could discern quite the disbelief in her tone, but of course that wasn't what I'd meant at all, and I said so at once.

"However," I added, "before I go on, I do wonder if it might be a good idea if someone were to call the police? Just on the off-chance that there has been some foul play afoot. One simply can't be *sure*."

Everyone had a little conflab, and it was decided that, since an ambulance had been called already, perhaps the police were on their way too, but it would be no harm to double check, so up got Kimberly again and went off to find out. Not a minute after that, she could be heard quite audibly, speaking on a telephone and clarifying that yes, an ambulance had been summoned, but yes, it seemed sensible to have the police come along too, just in case.

"Someone," Kimberly said, "has wondered if there might have been some 'foul play afoot'."

It is quite clear to the practised ear when another uses those little imaginary quote marks when they use someone else's words to relay a message, but in this instance, I was quite pleased she had done so, as it summed up the situation quite well for the purpose of the call, if you ask me.

"Yes," she said again, "in the Little Wittering library. Do ask them to come quickly, just in case."

I deduced that she must have been speaking on her mobile telephone because her voice loudened and I could make out the soft thuds of her footfall on the imitation wooden floor of the main section of the library, where one must suppose it was deemed impractical to use carpet, however hard-wearing a type one might select. As Kimberly neared, the response from the operator carried quite clearly down the line. I think it is fair to say that everyone in the room appeared to be holding their breath while trying to listen in, and the telephone voice agreed to send someone out immediately and asked if anyone were in any present danger.

"Er ... um ..." I expect Kimberly cast her gaze around us hopefully, as if we might either offer reassurance or fear, but of course I can't be certain of that.

Phyl said, "I shouldn't think so," just as Barbara said, "Perhaps there is a killer on the loose," in a most matter of fact way as if she were saying it may rain that afternoon, and that was enough for Mary to get a bit hysterical and squeal something about how if someone had killed Charlotte, maybe none of us were safe, so I didn't think Barbara had been altogether helpful in her comment.

Nonetheless, she did have a point as that very thought had crossed my mind, too, with the evidence I had gathered by that point. A little shiver of excitement and worry tingled up my spine all the way to the base of my neck and I gave a little shudder.

Phyl must have noticed, as she said, "Goose on your grave, Sal," and Kimberly said, "All right then, yes, I can do that, all right," and then after a moment where the operator spoke again, "Bye."

I hadn't been able to make out the operator's words that time, what with Mary crying and Barbara trying to make little jokes about it, which is her way of dealing with any kind of situation, and with Phyllis whispering about geese and graves and whatnot, but it didn't matter, because there was a faint *clck* which I presumed to be the operator disconnecting the call and then Kimberly told us what he'd said.

"He suggested we stay where we are and nobody leave. He said we would likely be asked some questions. Statements. Potential witnesses, maybe. Best to stay put."

"Some people may have already come and gone," Josephine said.

"Have we any way to find that out?" I said, with not much hope, as we had been far too busy chatting about poor Betty Barnard. Besides, most of us were not facing towards the main part of the library, and even if we had been, one's view is altogether limited by the angles and the bookshelves and the whatnots. Moreover, as I reminded the little group, one amongst us wouldn't be able to *see* anything more than a fuzzy greyness with the odd darker shadow or brighter patch, even had she been looking in the correct direction and paying any degree of attention to the goings on beyond our room.

Joan said in her feeble voice we'd better make that two of us, as she couldn't see very well herself, nowadays, so the others had better tell us about it immediately and spare no detail. Of course, everyone else muttered in agreement about taking turns to tell us what they could see, albeit in a somewhat convoluted manner as they all spoke at once, but I got the gist and I expect Joan did, too.

"Before we get started on that," I suggested to the group as a whole, "I wonder if one of us shouldn't see if we can secure the door to avoid any further coming or going while we await the arrival of the police."

"I'm sure she just collapsed ..." Josephine's words tailed off with an evident degree of uncertainty, so I supposed she was beginning to wonder if there had been a crime committed after all and wasn't at all as sure as she had said.

"It's just a precaution," I said, which was certainly the truth of the matter, regardless of whether it turned out to be necessary or not. "Why don't we spend our time waiting by doing one of our little observational exercises, only not with any reference to our book, but as a way of recording the events we have noticed in the library throughout the morning?" We are quite accustomed to doing these little exercises as we partake of our book discussions, and it had to be agreed that we all thoroughly enjoy the activity of it. "We are terribly good at extracting interesting details from our reading matter, so this should not be any great challenge to anyone of us. It may be useful to the police if it does turn out to be in anyway suspicious, and if not, then it will be a fun little exercise to hone our analytical skills."

"Our little grey cells," Joan said with some degree of delight in her frail voice. "What fun."

"Yes," I agreed. "Besides, *I* would very much like to know who and what everyone has seen and heard in the library throughout the morning, as I do find it awfully difficult to visualise something if no one has told me about it. I would be terribly grateful if each of you could describe what you can see from your chair, and have a little think about what you have seen throughout the morning; who you have spoken to aside from those of us within this room, and suchlike."

"Ah, good idea," said Phyllis, and patted the back of my hand with her own. I turned my hand over on the table and gave her a little squeeze, which I hope she interpreted as an instruction to help me along with finding out some details about who might have come into the library that morning and who might have left, and when any of them might have seen Charlotte beetling about the place doing her librarian duties, and what exactly those duties may have entailed.

"We'll use our notebooks to write it down."

"Good idea!"

"We'll be proper Poirots," Josephine said, and I have to admit I rather liked the idea of that.

"More like Miss Marple, some of us," Joan said in a bit of a quaver, but quite distinctly, and that gave us all a little chuckle. Joan's surname, you see, is Hickory, so we have already had the little joke about how we should do a Miss Marple next and she can read all the Miss Marple parts aloud, in the manner of dear old Joan Hicks. Whenever I listen to a Miss Marple audiobook, it is that wonderful lady's portrayal that I envisage in my mind, and despite no longer being able to see the television screen, Dennis and I do still enjoy putting on one of those older Agatha Christie's whenever one may appear on the viewing schedule. Dear old Joan Hicks is the very embodiment of Miss Marple, if you ask me, and Phyl and Joan Hickory and Josephine and I are all in perfect agreement about that.

Kimberly said she supposed she might as well go and talk to Carrie again about the door, as she'd already done about a thousand steps going back and forward and another trip would give her a few more. Kimberly is one of those people who likes to inform us of exactly how many steps she has walked in any given activity. Some time ago, she explained to me about a clever little watch contraption she has that can not only count her steps but also tells her about things such as her heart rate and BMI, which one has to admit is terribly useful and must save an awful lot of time waiting around in the doctor's surgery to be measured.

After a few moments, everyone settled into thinking about their observations of the morning, and aside from the scratching of pencils and gentle rumble of biros on paper, and the occasional sigh, there was little sound from any of us, so I, too, turned my mind to my account of things.

"I do hope it won't interrupt your thoughts if I whisper my notes to Phyllis," I said. The ladies are quite used to me either muttering into the recording contraption on my telephone or badgering dear Phyllis with my ideas, so they were quite gracious about it, and said they would treat it as a little background noise and do their best to filter it out and not let it influence them at all.

"Gary," I said to Phyl, and she tapped a finger on the back of my hand, which is our little code for, "I've got that, Sal, and I'll jot it down for you." If she presses on my index finger, it means, "say it again". A tap of my little finger means, "Wait a moment, Sal, I'm just writing a note," which she did next, and if she presses on my thumb, it means she'd already thought of that particular point. After a moment, she did press on my thumb, so I supposed she had been taking down a few extra details about Gary. Poor Gary is on the dole although he is terribly hard-working and has had quite the run of unfortunate luck. Even though he is quite accomplished at doing all kinds of handy odd jobs here and there, and Dennis assures me he did a perfectly adequate job of painting our fence, he has been finding it terribly difficult to get any permanent work. He pops into the library frequently to help with his job hunting, but it really doesn't appear to be doing him much good, I'm sorry to say.

Phyl tapped my little finger again, and hissed, "American," and I nodded to show her I knew what she meant, and didn't bother to add any more, as I could tell Phyl was writing about it from the soft scratching of her pen. I let her get on with it for a few moments, while I let my recollection of our arrival in the library play through my mind like one of those old-fashioned cine-films my mother used to show us on a Sunday afternoon.

Phyl and I had arrived at the library about fifteen minutes early, as we like to do, so that Phyllis can take the time to exchange her books. I usually have a little chat with Carrie while Phyllis is browsing, and if I am ready for a new audiobook, we sort that out too, but on that particular morning, I hadn't finished my borrowed book as I had been busy with *The ABC Murders* instead. Carrie and I were having a little chat about goodness knows what, and Charlotte was somewhere around the place as she said hello to us both as we came in and then scurried off somewhere to help someone who'd asked her about where to find a book about flower-arranging. It was about the time I was chatting with Carrie that the American came in, and I moved myself a little to the side and told her to go ahead with her inquiries as Carrie and I were simply passing the time of day while I was awaiting the start of our book club. The American said how quaint that sounded, and asked what we were reading, and I told her, and she said, "Ooh, how very English," and we had a little chuckle and then she said she was hoping to find out some local history about the place, and Carrie asked what in particular she wanted to know.

As it turned out, it was not so much a place she was interested in, but a person. She explained in quite some detail that she was trying to trace her birth family, as she had been given up for adoption as a baby and had been taken on by a wonderful American family and she was terribly grateful and had a perfectly wonderful life, but one always has that sense of curiosity about one's roots. I said I quite agreed and it must be terribly exciting, and like one of those treasure hunts one sometimes hears about, and I asked was this her first time in England and what successes had she had so far?

She said her name was April Kojoian, which is a most unusual name in Little Wittering, don't you agree? I recall it quite clearly and am quite certain about it, as Carrie said, "How do you spell that?" and the American woman spelled it out in a slow and careful manner with terribly precise enunciation, to be sure Carrie got it down correctly. She said she'd had an absolute plethora of names, through her life, and it wasn't the Kojoians she was searching for in Little Wittering. Carrie said what a shame, as anyone with a name like that would surely be easy to find, so I supposed she thought the same about it as had I. The American gave Carrie some more information, and said she was actually trying to trace more distant relations, as she thought her birth mother's family might have started out in the UK, and while Carrie was tapping away at her computer and making the odd little "hmm" or, "no, not that," or asking the odd question such as, "Is Mary Ellen with a hyphen or not?" I became quite engaged in the mystery, and then Phyl came back and joined in. Phyllis is my dearest friend, but I must tell you she is not one to hold back, and can be quite nosy once she takes an interest in a thing. She used to be a librarian until she retired in 2012, so I suppose that has something to do with it, and you won't be at all surprised to hear that she chipped in immediately and said Mary Ellen was an Irish name if you asked her, so it sounded very much as if April should look into those mother-and-baby homes in Ireland, as the timing matched quite well and perhaps that is how she'd originated. April said she was going to take a plane over to Dublin later in the week, and Phyl said she had a cousin in a little place in the middle of Ireland called Ballyfortnum, and maybe April should look her up as Linda did like to solve a mystery and it wouldn't be the first time she'd got involved in something like that.

Carrie said she'd send some information to the printer and it would cost April ten pence a sheet, and if she'd like to go and wait over by the printer, it should start popping out in a minute. Phyl and I wished her the best of luck, and off she went, just as the door opened with a gentle *squoosh* and a blast of air, and two other people came in at once.

I knew at once that it was Gary and Jeff who had entered, as Carrie greeted them both by name.

"The computers, is it?" she added after they'd done the pleasantries and the weather and whatnot.

"Please." I think it was Gary who said that, as his voice is quite deep and rough-sounding, as if he might be a smoker, although there is never any hint of cigarette about him, so perhaps he just has a naturally raspy voice or has given up. Jeff is an old student of mine, although he must be at least forty by now and works as a window cleaner. He said, "Morning Mrs S.," then told Carrie he was just dropping off his wife's books before they got on with the windows, and Carrie said he could have left them in the deposit box, and he said he hadn't known about that and Carrie said, "Well now you do," but she said it in a perfectly pleasant way and not at all sarcastically. She said she'd show him, and off he went around the desk and out the other door, and off went Carrie with him.

While Carrie was out in the lobby showing him the box, in came Joan and Barbara, together, as they quite often do, and Phyl and I went with them to the meeting room, although I went via the lavatories, just to be sure. Whilst I was therein, I quickly realised Charlotte was installed in the neighbouring cubicle. There are only two, so the area is quite compact, with just the usual thin partitions dividing one from another so of course I could hear every sound. I must say she had quite a conversation on her mobile telephone as she was doing her business, which I find most unsavoury and I do hope she gave the telephone a good wipe while she was washing her hands, but I was finished and out again by then so I will just have to imagine that she did. I returned at once to the meeting room, and as the rest of the book club ladies had arrived by then, we settled down to get on with it, and that was that.

"Okay, who else was there when we came in?" Phyl asked, giving me a little nudge. I had been so caught up in it all that I hadn't noticed she had finished writing and awaited my next observation. I told her what I'd thought of, and she said she'd quite forgotten about Jeff coming in, which just goes to show that you don't need to be blessed with good eyesight to notice things, but then she said she'd noticed a young woman already stationed by the computers, and two men browsing amongst the bookshelves, but all three were awfully quiet and had left soon after, so it was no wonder I hadn't known about them. Then she said surely I couldn't have forgotten the mother with the small child in the children's section, as he was making quite the noise, and she had a point as I had completely overlooked the pair of them, but I said I doubted very much that a two-year-old had killed anyone.

Phyl huffed a bit and said his mother might have done, which I had to concede was a possibility. "She didn't though," Phyl went on. "They left just after we came into the meeting room, while you had nipped off to the loo. Barbara and I had just got Joan settled, and the child ran across to the desk. The mother caught him up and got a hold of him, and Carrie said goodbye to them and if her tone of voice was anything to go by, I'd say she was glad to see the back of them. I presume they went out, so, as we'd have heard a bit from him if not, sure we would."

"How did everyone else get on?" I asked, directing my voice to encompass the rest of the group. The other ladies had begun to chatter a little too, so I supposed they must have finished making their own lists.

Kimberly had come back whilst we were in the middle of writing our lists, but she said why didn't everyone else go first and then she'd see if she could add anything she'd spotted from her excursions running about the place like a mad-woman, and we all conceded that was a good idea.

Josephine said why don't we start with Phyllis, and work our way clockwise around the table, which would leave Kimberly until last. One can tell that Josephine has experience of working in schools, as it was a very sensible and logical suggestion and we all agreed immediately.

Phyl and I shared our notes, although Phyllis did most of the talking as it were she who could read the notes, and Josephine said we make quite the team. Phyl went through it quickly enough, and said that was that, as neither of us had paid much attention to whatever might be going on beyond the meeting room, once our book talk had begun. We'd both been seated with our backs to the room, and were giving our full commitment to the discussion, so it wasn't at all unusual that we hadn't be paying attention to anything beyond. I added that Amity hadn't noticed anyone untoward, either, or she would most certainly have alerted me to the fact, as she is trained to do. Aside from that, there was one piece of information I was keeping to myself for the time being, as I didn't want to put a cat among the pigeons, as one might say.

Besides, I did hope I might get an opportunity to discuss it with Phyllis to see if she agreed that it might be somewhat suspicious, in light of the circumstances and before I said it to the rest of them.

It was Joan's turn to go next, and she said in her thin, fragile voice that she would be able to see all the way across to the computers if it wasn't for the library being full of bookshelves. We all had another little chuckle, and then she said she really hadn't been paying any kind of attention, and her eyesight is not what it used to be. "I can't see much more than Sally, nowadays, dears. I wouldn't be able to say who came in or out." She laid her papery-skinned hand over mine to show me she was having a joke with me, although the pressure was so light it were as if a bird had alighted briefly. She hadn't much more to say, after that, so we moved quickly around to the next person at the table, which was Barbara, but she said she really hadn't anything of importance, and why didn't we jump on to the next person just in case we ran out of time. Josephine said it was a very sensible idea, which goes to show that she and Barbara are quite friendly and don't bicker all the time.

Josephine said she hadn't anything to add either, and she quite agreed with Barbara about moving on quickly, "Mary has the best view," Josephine said, "so perhaps we should let her go next, just in case the police arrive soon and put a stop to our chattering about it."

Of course once Barbara and Josephine agreed with each other, everyone else agreed quite easily that Mary *was* the person with the most useful view of the room. She sat in the corner facing into the library and could see a large portion of the desk and computer section as there was a wide break in the bookshelves, creating an aisle down the centre of the library. She said the angle of her seat was such that she had an almost clear path to the section of the desk that faces into the room, and onwards past the desk to the photocopier and computers. "Of course," she said, with a little giggle, "there are some lower shelves and suchlike in the way, and the desk does block some of the computer bit, but I would think anyone would have to pass through that area at some point between coming in and going out, unless they went out through the entrance door."

"You can't," said Josephine. "The door only opens one way."

"Unless someone holds it open so one can nip out the wrong way," Barbara said, and we agreed it was possible but didn't happen very often as Carrie was a stickler for it and had a tendency to call out and put a stop to it.

"It messes up the people-counter," she'd explain, whenever the need arose. I once asked her what on earth she was talking about, and she took the time to explain that there is a sensor on the exit door that counts how many people leave the building, which gathers data to prove the usage of the library, which I thought was a terribly nifty little device. After that, Phyl and I always made a point of exiting separately, one after the other, to be sure it counted us both. Besides, it was a useful exercise for Amity to get the practice of negotiating the doorway without Phyllis helping us.

However, just as Mary started to tell us about anything she had noticed during the morning, Barbara's prediction that we may not have sufficient time to get through everyone was proved accurate, as there was the screech of a siren, followed by a pounding at the door, so I guessed that either the police or the paramedics had arrived on the scene.

Kimberly said, "I'll go," in quite a resigned manner. She must have already been getting to it, because as she spoke, her chair scraped on the carpet, and the rose-scent wafted once more. As it turned out, it wasn't necessary for her to get up after all, as before she got very much further, there was a swoosh and soft draught so I knew at once someone else had beaten Kimberly to it.

We all fell silent to listen and Carrie said, "Thank goodness. You'd better come in."

Chapter Four

It appeared to be the paramedics and not the police, as one of the first things they said was, "Did anyone call the police?" to which Carrie said yes, someone had kindly done that for her.

"Poor Charlotte is just over here but I'm afraid it might be too late." Carrie is usually the kind of person who is very calm and measured, and it was quite unusual to pick up any kind of tremor in her tone, so she must have had quite the shock.

As far as I could tell, there was a male paramedic and a female paramedic, unless one of them had an uncommonly deep voice for a woman, or vice versa. The female one said something about how she would go with Carrie, whom she seemed to know so I wondered if she were a regular visitor to the library, or if they might know each other from elsewhere, but it hardly seemed to be of importance so I didn't dwell on it. "You grab the trolley, eh George?" she said, her voice becoming louder as she advanced further into the library.

The door swished and swooshed so I guessed the male paramedic was doing as his colleague suggested, while she bustled along after Carrie to attend to poor Charlotte, and Phyl and I clasped each other's arms and the book club ladies sat in breath-bated silence.

"Shall I carry on?" Mary asked eventually.

"Yes please," I said, "as there doesn't seem to be much else we can do."

For not the first time, I was thoroughly impressed at how observant Mary seems to be. I would have been quite happy to have had her in any one of my English classes throughout my time at St Cuthbert's, and had said as much to her on more than one occasion. She scuttled through an account of a few people who had come and gone, which seemed of little importance as she said that both Carrie and Charlotte had been at the desk for most of that time, and if either of them had left to go anywhere, they had come back fast enough. She'd only noticed one person who'd come in and not gone out. "There was that dishy bloke Charlotte used to see, who'd gone over into the computers. I think he must be still there unless I missed him, but I don't think I would've because he's totes bloomin' gorgeous."

I didn't bother to ask about what she meant by 'totes' as one could tell from the way she drew out the vowels exactly what she thought of the young man in question.

Then Isobel said, "He's Harry," in a dreamy kind of way, and Kimberly said, "Ooh, he *is* lovely isn't he?"

Mary said, "Mmm," and she, like Isobel, was quite wistful about it. "Bel's hot for him."

"Aren't we all?" Kimberly said, at the same time as Josephine said, "Don't blame you, love," and I wished for a fleeting moment that I might be able to see this vision they were swooning about. Nevertheless, they seemed to have got rather off track, and as my ears had pricked up at the link to Charlotte, I asked Mary if this wonderful Harry person was the last to come in and she said, no, that was three of her friends rushing in together, asking something at the desk, collecting up an armful of books, and dashing onwards. "They're at college," she said, by way of explanation. "Hilary is doing English, so I expect the books were for her as the others would use the academic library on campus."

Isobel piped up and added that Hilary was in her group and one of the others was a friend of hers, too, and she'd given them a wave, but they'd gone out straight away, which confirmed Mary's account of things quite nicely.

I said I was inclined to agree with her about the books, and asked her whether she could recall whether it had been Carrie or Charlotte her friends had spoken to.

"Charlotte," Mary said without any hesitation, so I asked her if she happened to have any clarity as to what time that might have been.

She couldn't be sure, but she said it must have been a good while ago, as she'd seen Charlotte after that, talking to other customers and answering the phone, and rushing back and forth with books and papers and suchlike.

"And did she look well?" It is not uncommon for Phyllis to say the precise thing that is on my mind, so I wasn't at all surprised. We know each other terribly well and she is very attuned to my thoughts.

"Seemed okay to me," Mary said. "She looked about the same as ever. Lippy done. Not a hair out of place."

"Barbie doll," Barbara muttered, and Mary gave the tiniest of giggles.

"Yes, that describes her quite well, doesn't it." Josephine said, and Joan said it certainly did, and I must say it matched my impression of Charlotte as she always sounded like the type of person who was somewhat self-obsessed and spent far too much time thinking about her appearance, if you ask me.

Barbara once described Charlotte as one of those stereotypical movie librarians, in the scenes after the top buttons are undone, the spectacles are removed and the hair let down. Phyllis had chuckled but said that was hardly fair as Charlotte wears glasses all the time and is very well-suited to them and she is nice enough when you get to know her.

Barbara had disagreed about that, saying she was a bit of a troublemaker in more ways than one, and too high-and-mighty for her own good. Phyl had disagreed with that too, but Phyl is the kind of person who sees the best in someone, even if they are the type to go around stealing lollipops from children, but that's Phyl for you. I'm digressing, of course, as Mary didn't say anything about Charlotte's character and only took great care in telling us what she had seen her doing, which wasn't anything of great significance, she said, with a little sigh as if she had hoped to have noticed something of interest. "She went off with the older bloke for a bit, went over to the computers, fiddled around at something by the photocopier, moved some books about the place ... nothing much. Disappeared out of sight for a while, or I stopped looking or didn't notice ... I suppose that's it," she said, with another sigh. "She seemed totes normal, acting totes normal, and doing all her totes normal things."

"Who did you *last* see her talking to?" I asked, wondering if that might give us a little something to go on.

"She was over in the computers, but I can't really see all the way into that bit, because the desk and the shelves and anyone standing at the counter are in the way. And if she moved into non-fic or the other room or any of that kind of thing, I wouldn't see her at all."

I imagine she gave a little shrug at that, because her voice lifted a fraction as she said it, but it wasn't any kind of a question, so we left it at that and Kimberly said as Ashwini still hadn't come back we might as well hear if Barbara and Josephine were quite sure they hadn't anything at all to add before going on to Isobel and then that would just leave her to fill any gaps unless Ashwini got back to us before that.

Barbara said she hadn't really paid any attention at all to anything much as she was chatting to us and thinking about the book and what she might buy for her tea on her way home, so she wasn't very much use at all. "I came in with Joan – you were at the desk with Phyllis, remember – passed Jeff on his way out and Carrie was fiddling about in the lobby with the deposit box, and I came over and helped Joan get settled and that was about it because then Josephine came and we got chatting."

I nudged Phyl, and I hoped she understood what I was trying to convey, because although while I imagine that even Doofus Finbury might be fractionally more observant than Barbara, she had reminded me of something that might be quite helpful. Phyllis nudged me back, so I think that meant she'd got it, and before either of us said anything, Josephine said something else that reminded me of another piece of information that may turn out to be useful if one were to get the chance to act upon it:

"I came in, opened the windows, said hello, put my bag down, and went off to put the kettle on." Josephine is very good at taking care of the tea, even when it isn't her turn on the rota. It should have been Nora, but she hadn't come, so I expect Josephine noticed that and set about sorting it out rather than making a fuss about who should do it instead. Josephine is awfully practical like that, which I suppose comes from years of working with the most unpredictable of students, or perhaps it is the other way around and she is good at her job because of being a practical kind of person who isn't at all fazed by a setback.

"Josephine," I said, when she had finished talking, "are the window cleaners still here?"

A few people spoke at the same time, and it seemed to be a mixture of uncertainty and probability, and Barbara said something about Schrödinger's window cleaners which made everyone chuckle quite loudly – well, except poor Kimberly who said what on earth was she on about, so she had to explain, but I must say I thought it was terribly witty. After we had told Kimberly all about it, she said she supposed she could get up yet again and see if there was any sign of them anywhere. There was the scape of a chair moving on the carpet and a heavy sigh, so I gathered she wasn't exactly keen about the idea but had got herself moving nonetheless.

"So over to you, Bel," Josephine said. "What have you got to add to the party?"

You may have noticed that we are quite divided in how we address the newest member of our book club. Isobel is friendly with Mary, and they usually arrive together, and refer to each other as Mares and Bel, and after some time, Barbara and Kimberly picked up on it. When she'd first come along, a few months ago, Josephine had said she'd known Isobel since she was quite small and been called anything from Bella to Bel-bel to Baby Bel and back again. Barbara had said that was terribly cheesy and that gave us all a good laugh, although Joan said she'd never quite got the hang of those funny Dutch cheeses and what was wrong with a nice bit of Cheddar, so I suppose everyone has different taste, when it comes to cheese, but that's hardly the point, is it?

Isobel said she hadn't seen anyone much, except when she'd nipped out to the loo, and she thought Carrie and Charlotte had both been at the desk but she couldn't be sure. She said she hadn't really paid any attention to who might have been in the library or not, but there was someone with a baby because she'd had to step out of the way to let the pram get through. Then she said there might have been a couple of people bashing away at the computers, which was at odds with her story because the computers are on the opposite side of the library and not at all close to the lavatories, and I couldn't imagine how she would notice the tapping of keys if she hadn't noticed anything closer.

I didn't say anything but I paid good attention to what else Isobel had to say for herself, because she was one of only two of our little Book Club group who had left the meeting room at any point during our get-together, and it hadn't escaped my notice that even though she had said she was nipping to the lavatory, she had not passed behind my chair as she would have had to do to get to the Ladies. She had been gone for quite a while, and when she returned, she smelled faintly of those fiddly rolled-up cigarettes, so I supposed she'd gone out for a smoke, but why didn't she say so?

"Are you quite sure you didn't see anything else useful?" I turned my face towards where I believed Isobel sat, as far as I could discern from her voice. "You are the only one of us, other than Josephine, who left the room before Carrie called for assistance, so you might have the most pertinent information." I didn't mention that I was quite certain she had *not* used the lavatories, but had gone in quite the opposite direction, as I didn't want to alert her to the fact that I had noticed. Isobel is quite new to the group and has only been coming along for a few months, and she was not a former pupil of St Cuthbert's, so we didn't know each other particularly well. I rather hoped on this occasion that she might underestimate my senses, and have me pegged as a somewhat doddery blind old bat, although as I hadn't done anything to give her that impression previously, I wasn't sure I would get away with the ruse.

I patted my foot around until I found Phyl's foot, and gave her a little poke, to let her know I was onto something, and she pushed her foot up into mine in response. While I was at it, I gave Amity a little rub with the ball of my foot, and she huffed and rolled over, and went back to sleep beneath the table as if she were terribly bored with the whole situation.

Isobel didn't say anything for a moment or two, so I gathered she was either thinking about what she might have seen, or thinking about what she might say, and I was wondering whether the two might be the same or at odds. After quite a pause, she said, "I suppose Harry was still there, and that other bloke, and a curly-haired woman ... and Carrie was busy on the telephone, I think. I really can't be sure, I was hardly paying attention, was I?"

"Did you only go to the loo?" Phyllis asked innocently. "Sure, didn't you come in from the other direction, after, or was that someone else?"

"Yeah, Bel, she's right! You'd nipped out for a smoke, hadn't you? An' to get a look at gorgeous Harry, most like." There was the movement of a chair as Kimberly spoke, and a soft thump on the other side of Phyllis, so it seemed as if Kimberly had returned and caught the end of the conversation about what Isobel had or hadn't been up to.

I was most uncertain as to whether Kimberly's little interjection was of more help or hindrance, to be perfectly honest. I was grateful that she had confirmed my suspicions about Isobel but I would have much preferred Isobel to have offered the confession about the smoking without the idea being put into her mind, in case there was more to it, as it were.

Isobel didn't say anything for a second or two and then took a little breath as if she might be feeling caught in the act about something. "Yes, I did, but I know some people disapprove, so I wasn't going to mention it."

I must say she sounded terribly put out about it, although I couldn't be certain whether it was because she had been caught in a mistruth or whether she was still concealing the full story of where exactly she had been when she was not, in fact, visiting the lavatory. At just about the moment I was wondering about asking her more about it, Kimberly spoke first.

"The window cleaners must be doing the high-up window at the side of the building," she said. "I saw the ladder through the glass."

I couldn't see how this was connected to Isobel and whether or not she had been to the lavatories, but nonetheless, it did show a certain degree of attention to detail on Kimberley's part, don't you agree? It was of little surprise that Kimberly had the most to say about anything, as she had been up and down to see what was going on and hadn't yet managed to report back very well at all, what with all the interruptions and the paramedics and whatnot, so I think it is safe to presume we were all quite keen to hear what she had to tell us. She was just getting into it when there was yet another kerfuffle in the main room and Mary said it looked like the paramedics had poor Charlotte all loaded up and ready to go.

"They aren't moving in any great hurry," she said, in that hushed and dramatic tone one hears in a film when something sombre is underway. "The man is pushing the stretcher thing, Sally, but he's not paying much attention to Charlotte, only trying not to bump into the bookshelves." Mary is one of those rare young people in Little Wittering who addresses me by my Christian name, and I must say it always catches me off guard, as it is quite uncommon when one has been a teacher around the vicinity for so long, but Mary is younger, so I suppose she has simply never thought of me in that way. Nonetheless, it was terribly kind of her to tell me what was going on, and I was reminded of what a pleasant and personable young woman she must be, don't you agree? So I suppose it is of little matter, and Phyl is often saying it's the modern way, although I wonder if it hasn't more to do with my having been retired for so long that an entire generation has grown up without my presence in St Cuthbert's. It gives me quite the pang, if I dwell on it.

"The girl one's just strolling along chatting to Carrie," Mary said, "so I suppose Charlotte really must be dead." With that, her voice broke up and she gave another little sob and there was a push of a chair and a bit of rustling and fussing and Josephine saying, "Oh dear, come on now, it's all right," even though we were fairly certain that it wasn't all right for Charlotte, at least, but it was kind of Josephine to try.

While Josephine was fussing over Mary, Isobel said, "That man has got up to get the door. Big man, beard. Looks like a lorry driver?"

I thought for a moment and deduced she must mean Gary, although as far as I am aware, he has never driven a lorry. He does have one of those vans with quite the miscellany of tools stashed within, in case he is called upon to complete any odd jobs here and there, which I suppose is a similar sort of thing in terms of having a beard. Phyllis hadn't said anything about him leaving, so I supposed he had been *in situ*, as it were, throughout the hour or so since Book Club had begun. I added him to my mental list of people closer to the action who might be able to throw a little more light on the subject.

"Sally," Barbara said, as there was a little lull in the observations whilst the paramedics removed poor Charlotte from the library, "you haven't said why you think someone might have killed her, and I don't know about everyone else, but I'd quite like to hear it."

There was a murmur of agreement, and I thought for a moment or two about how much or how little I should say. I didn't want to alarm anyone, or put anyone in a difficult spot, so I took a little breath to gather my thoughts and said, "I happened to overhear some information that gives me cause to suspect it. I must tell you I was not alarmed at the time, as I presumed it to be a manner of speaking. Blowing off some steam, as we used to say. I did not presume it to bear any accuracy of the speaker's words."

Someone said, "Who?" and someone else said, "Go on."

I ignored the former and attended to the latter. "Upon my arrival this morning, I visited the Ladies. I usually do so before we settle down for our copious amounts of tea. I find it far more convenient to get it over and done with before I take my seat than to have the hoohah of getting up and negotiating it all later, and I'm sure you can understand the sense in that. Amity and I were negotiating our way into the cubicle – they are a little tight, don't you agree?"

"They are indeed," Joan said, in her croaky voice. "I can be gone for a wet Wednesday if I hit the door frame." I supposed she meant with her walking frame, and everyone chuckled sympathetically and Josephine said they really must get a disabled toilet sorted and I said they do have one, but it's off through the staff bit and the trip is quite the effort in itself. Joan agreed, and then one of the others, who I think was probably Isobel but I couldn't be quite sure about that said, "What did you hear, Sally?"

I had lost my train of thought so I had a little think to remember where I'd got to, and said Amity and I were just getting ourselves settled when it came to my attention someone else was also in the lavatories. Talking. At first, I presumed the person to be speaking to me in the way one sometimes does when in a public lavatory and I expected to be asked if I wouldn't mind passing some tissue over the door, or suchlike, but then I realised she was not, in fact, talking to me, but into a telephone.

"She was chattering away, and I must say I find it most unnerving that one might make use of one's telephone whilst relieving oneself. It seems terribly unhygienic, and rather unpleasant for the recipient of one's call, one would imagine, but I suppose that is by the by."

Barbara said sometimes it's the only time she gets any peace to have a chat with anyone, and Kimberly said imagine having three small children, and I could see her point about that, although I still disagreed.

"Nonetheless," I said, after we'd argued it out for a moment, "I thought little of the conversation at the time, of course, as I was concentrating on my own affairs. However, now it seems apparent poor Charlotte might be dead, I've remembered rather more detail of the telephone conversation, of which I am reluctant to share at present."

There was a bit of a sigh, which I attributed to more than one person about the table, so I supposed they felt I had somehow let them down. "One simply does not wish to cast aspersions when one can't be entirely certain as to which parts of the information are relevant, and which are merely red herrings, as it were. Suffice to say that there is more than one person present in this library whom I believe Charlotte disliked, or whom she felt may dislike her, and it is not a great leap to suppose one of them might wish her harm."

"But ..."

"Who ..."

"What ..."

Several of the ladies around the table spoke at once, so of course I couldn't discern who was saying what, or what exactly it was that any of them wanted to know, so I said nothing and waited it out.

They fell silent again, and then Josephine spoke into the void. "There's quite the difference between disliking a person and killing them, Sal."

"Nonetheless, she is dead, and that is exactly why we must proceed with caution."

It certainly didn't seem prudent to suggest that one of the people in question was seated at this very table.

Chapter Five

The paramedics called goodbye to Carrie and suggested she might get herself a nice cup of tea for the shock and close up early, but she reminded them that the police were yet to arrive on the scene and they said, just the cup of tea then, and perhaps a biscuit or two, and the exit door swished closed and silence fell over the library once more.

A moment or two later, the silence was broken by someone asking if they could leave, as they really needed to be on their way, and poor Carrie sighed and said she really didn't know, to be honest.

Josephine said she'd get up and see if she could help Carrie with that, and off she went, leaving the rest of us to think about things for a bit longer.

"Where *are* the police?" Kimberly said, and Barbara made the kind of comment I didn't like to repeat, although I must say I was in perfect agreement with the sentiments, but then Phyllis said quite calmly that someone dying quietly in the library might not be as high priority as something like a bank robbery or a traffic accident. Barbara said she supposed so, and although I thought a murder might be of greater importance, I didn't say it aloud as there seemed little point in adding to any sense of worry about the situation and no one seemed to be entirely convinced that we did in fact have a murder in the midst of things, except me.

Kimberly huffed and said it would probably only be useless Finbury anyway, so he might as well not bother, and I said, "Oh, yes, weren't you in his year at school?" and she said yes, she had been, and she hadn't got over it yet. Of course, that gave us a bit of a chuckle, although it was a fair observation as he has a terribly irritating way about him. I said that in my opinion, he would have been far better suited to another career in which he was not expected to deal with the public.

"Such as a sewer inspector?" Barbara said, so she must know him too.

"I'm going to make that tea." Josephine spoke behind me and gave me quite the start, as even though she is usually terribly heavy on her feet, I had been lost in my thoughts and not heard a sound. "And I've told Carrie to come and sit in here with us, but she says she ought to stay at the desk, so perhaps some of us should keep her company. I'll fill the kettle up and we'll all have one."

This gave me an awfully good idea and I said as much to everyone around the table without giving too much away. "Why don't we *all* take a little breather? I'm quite sure Carrie would appreciate a little distraction and I know Phyllis here was rather hoping she might catch that American again before she disappears off on her travels."

"I –"

I was quite certain Phyllis was about to say she had hoped nothing of the sort, so I gave her a little nudge with my foot and she got the idea and shut up. I pushed back my chair, took up Amity's harness, and gave her the command to guide me. "Besides," I added for good measure, "poor Amity must be getting awfully stiff, so she would like a little stretch about and an opportunity to have a sniff of some of the delicious library smells."

"Like pee in the children's corner? Or dead bodies?" Barbara said in that dry way of hers so one can't be sure whether she is having a joke or not.

"Precisely," I retorted, in my sweet little-old-lady voice. Then I lowered my tone to a dramatic whisper that reminded me very much of a particularly outstanding sixth-form production of Macbeth in 2007. "Or murderers."

She laughed, and said she either hoped not, or hoped so, depending on whether there was a murderer to find, in which case she hoped Amity would sniff him out, or no murderer, which she hoped more even though it wouldn't have the same excitement.

"Now do come along, Phyl, let's go and see how the American is bearing up amongst this quaint English village murder mystery she has stumbled upon. I expect she will either be finding it terribly thrilling or terribly tiresome."

Phyl got to her feet, although she was a little slow about it so I sensed some reluctance and gave her a little prod with my fingers to convey some sense of urgency. She bucked up a bit at that and slipped her arm into mine, and thus, the three of us – Phyllis, Amity, and I – started on our way from the meeting room towards the computer section, where I guessed the American remained.

Not a moment later, Phyl said, "There she is," and speeded up, so I was pleased my instincts had been correct about it.

Before she could tug me off balance, I said, "Slow down a minute, Phyllis, you'll cause quite the accident." She slowed immediately and I tugged her closer towards me so I could whisper, "Of course I am perfectly capable of keeping up, even at that pace, but I need you to be my eyes before we get any further. Are we alone?"

Phyllis immediately stopped walking, but didn't answer me straight away so I suspect she had a little look around to assess the situation before committing one way or the other. After a moment of scoping out the library, she whispered, "Yes, I think so. What is it, and what on earth is it that has got you all bee-in-bonnet?"

"Is that good-looking young man still here? The one Isobel and Kimberly were getting all excited about?"

"Wasn't it Joan and Mary? Hang on ..." She gave my arm a little jerk upwards as she moved, and I wondered if she might be popping her head out from behind a bookshelf in just the manner of one of the cartoon characters who disappear behind a tree to spy upon their prey. "Yes," she said a moment later, "he's at the computer in the corner, but he doesn't seem to be doing anything with it. Miles away, sure he is, gazing off into nothing, by the look of him."

"And who else is still here?"

"April – you know, the American you're so keen for us to get at. She's at the one by the window. And Gary. On the middle one. That's it, I think, although there might be others lurking in the bookshelves."

"Who is at the desk with Carrie? I can hear Josephine and Mary, I think?"

"Josephine, Kimberly, Ashwini. Not Mary, she's chattering to Isobel in the meeting room still, I should think. Here comes Barbara too now, with a plate of biscuits. Shall I get you one of the Maryland or a plain Digestive?"

I'd quite forgotten about Ashwini, what with all the hoohah and excitement, and it caused me quite the flutter of worry that I may have forgotten someone else. I stood frozen in thought while Barbara and Phyl had a bit of a conflab about the biscuits and then Phyl pressed one of chocolate chip cookies into my hand and said I seemed to have lost my tongue so she'd chosen for me, and of course she had got it quite right. I gave myself a little mental shake and said thank you and perhaps if the other meeting room were empty, we should pop into there for a minute to eat our biscuits because we wouldn't want to spray crumbs all over the computers or any of those other electrical contraptions, would we?

Phyl said it seemed like a sensible idea, and asked if she should get a Digestive for Amity, to which I said no, I shouldn't think so.

She steered me to a chair, and although the right-hand meeting room is almost identical in size and shape to the one from which we had just come, as I think I may have mentioned, it has quite a different feel to it, which I expect comes from the window not opening, as it smelled terribly musty and stuffy and was awfully hot.

"Phyl," I said, once we had sat, "the thing is, Charlotte has had a bit of a falling out with the dishy young man, if he is who I believe him to be. I heard her discussing it on her telephone. She said he simply won't leave her alone, since she broke off their relationship, and he was here in the library *again*, and she put the most enormous amount of emphasis on the *again* part, and then there was a bit of a pause while the person on the other end spoke, and I didn't catch that at all, as I don't like to eavesdrop."

Phyl gave one of her snorts, but I ignored the interruption and carried on, as I've found it entirely more sensible to simply ignore her when she gets like that.

"There was a bit of tinkling noise, as we were doing our business, and well, I'm sure you agree that when one is divided only by the thinnest of cubicle walls, and they reach neither the floor nor the ceiling, one simply can't help but overhear, especially when a person is becoming quite heated about a jilted lover."

Phyl gave a little gasp of excitement, and said that would explain why the lovely young man looked so wistful and crestfallen, wouldn't it, and I said she mustn't think of him as lovely if he turned out to be the kind of person who might follow someone around in an unsettling and sinister kind of a manner, especially if the poor girl had made her intentions perfectly clear.

"Oh, like one of those stalkery yokes," Phyl said, and I said exactly. She was silent for a beat, and then she said, "Ooh. Not lovely, so, sure he's not. But he is a dish." She was quiet again for a moment, and then she said, "You said more than one, Sal?"

"More than one?"

"More than one person here who might want to harm Charlotte?"

Of course, she was perfectly correct, and I wasn't at all surprised, as Phyllis is the kind of person who is most attentive to details, and once she'd clarified that it wasn't more than one stalker-type person in our midst, or more than one biscuit to which she referred, I agreed at once. "Yes."

"Well, you daft woman, who?"

"Phyllis, if you had been paying any attention at all, you would be able to guess at once. Think about it."

I suppose she did as I suggested, because she didn't say anything for a few seconds, although I suppose she may have simply been enjoying her chocolate chip cookie or whichever of the biscuits she had chosen for herself, although I do know Phyllis terribly well so I would be very surprised if it was the plain Digestive. Regardless, after a moment, she said, "Do you mean Carrie?"

I said I hadn't meant Carrie at all, but if she thought it a good idea, perhaps we should add Carrie to the list of those with the motive and opportunity and she said of course we should, as it was perfectly obvious that Carrie had not forgiven Charlotte for the usurping.

"Whatever do you mean?" I said, with quite some surprise. "Isn't that all water under the bridge?"

"Goodness no! If you could only see the darting looks of rage Carrie shoots towards Charlotte whenever she isn't watching, Sal, you'd know exactly what I mean."

I have to admit I was quite taken aback by this revelation as I had been under the impression that Carrie didn't mind too much at all about the promotion, once the initial disappointment had passed. Any time in which the subject had arisen, Carrie had agreed she would be retiring in a couple more years anyway so perhaps it was for the best, but as Phyl relayed her own observations of the matter, I wondered if I might have missed some terribly important visual clues. I must admit I felt an awful pang of remorse that I may not have realised poor Carrie might have terribly upset about the whole affair after all.

"Could you be at all mistaken? If my memory is accurate, Carrie does have a somewhat dour face about her, although I suppose she may have got over it by now, so I wouldn't be inclined to read much into it. She does take her job very seriously as she is quite the professional, don't you agree?"

Phyl said she did see what I meant, and Carrie does have a rather unfortunate stern manner about her, but she would bet her last chocolate chip cookie there was no love lost between the pair of them – Carrie and Charlotte, that was.

I reminded her she had already eaten the cookie and she said not to be such an eejit which is a terribly Irish expression that usually makes me giggle, but I was too busy thinking about whether Carrie might have wished ill harm to poor Charlotte so I simply asked if there was any other evidence that Carrie might have been pushed so far as to commit a murder?

Phyl said wasn't having a young pretender come along and take the job you'd been working towards for the last twenty years quite enough?

I did have a little giggle about that. Although I have never actually *seen* Charlotte, of course, I had been quite aware that she does not take the same level of pride in her job as Carrie. Charlotte, I had always suspected, was rather too inclined towards idle gossip and passing the buck whenever she could, so Phyllis's description of Charlotte as a young pretender was perfectly accurate if you ask me.

"Only last week I asked her to see if she couldn't find out when the next Janice Hallet would be released and she said Carrie would know and she called over to Carrie and asked would she just look it up and give me the information. I got the distinct impression that Charlotte wasn't doing anything at all important and could have performed the task perfectly well herself if only she'd put her mind to it, so I suppose you have a point. Perhaps there was a burning resentment loitering under the surface."

"Not so far under, if you could only see the looks," Phyl said again, with quite some feeling.

I gave her a little nod to show I was listening, and added Carrie to the list of suspects I was building in my mind, albeit with some reluctance as I know Carrie quite well and didn't like to think she may have bashed Charlotte about the head and killed her in cold blood. Of course, I didn't know if anyone *had* been bashed about the head and imagined that might not be the case as we would have heard the commotion. Moreover, I am certain Amity would have alerted us all to that level of violence in such close proximity.

"Well then, if we include Carrie as a suspect, we have at least three people to consider," I said to Phyl. "I think it would be a very good idea if we were to go and ask a few pertinent questions of some of the witnesses while we have the chance."

"Three?" Phyl said. "We have the dishy young Harry, and Carrie, but who is the third? You are being awfully secretive, Salamander Smith."

As I was already on my feet and being led towards the computers by darling Amity, I merely whispered, "Isobel, of course," and continued on my way.

Chapter Six

The soft whirring of the computers and the tapping of keys told me we had reached that particular section of the library, so I said to Phyllis, "Lead me to the American woman, if you would."

Phyl said she was just over by the window, so if I stepped to the right to avoid crashing into the photocopier again, and then took about six steps forward, she'd lead me around the table and then we'd be in about the right place.

I reminded her that particular incident with the photocopier had only happened once, and several years ago, after the man who had serviced the infernal contraption had left it out of place, and that Amity was perfectly capable of avoiding a machine of that size and wasn't she a blessing. Phyl said she'd quite forgotten it had happened before Amity had arrived, and I said well there you are then. Side by side, we moved nearer to the brightness that told me we were approaching the window, and the American woman said, "Oh, hi there."

Before we had a chance to respond, someone pounded heartily on the door of the library.

Phyllis said a word that I will not repeat, as it was perfectly uncouth, but a minute or two later, the relative quiet of the library was shattered by the jumped-up tones of a voice I knew all too well.

"What's going on here then?"

It became immediately clear why Phyllis had uttered that particular word, and I must say I agreed with her completely. "Oh, for goodness sake," I muttered to Phyl. "Could they really not have sent one of the more competent officers along?"

She gave one of her little huffs and Police Constable Finbury said quite loudly and in a terribly unpleasant manner from somewhere over near the desk, "Who are all these people and where is the deceased?"

Someone gave a heavy sigh and I suppose it might have been Carrie as she was next to speak. "Constable Finbury," she said, in the usual unenthusiastic tones of anyone who has met this particular individual before. I expected her to continue, but of course the imbecile interrupted her before she had the chance, and I thought that if Phyllis were correct about the dangers of Carrie's covert stares towards her recently-departed colleague, perhaps she could direct such a glare towards Doofus Finbury and see if she couldn't manage to polish him off while she was at it. I gave myself a little shake. I am really not the kind of person to wish ill upon another, even if that person is Doofus Finbury, implausibly graduated from Police Training College or wherever it is one sends delinquents such as he to train for the police these days.

Of course, the idiotic child's name is not really Doofus Finbury, although it is a name to which he is perfectly suited. His given name is Dougal Rufus Finbury, so one can see how it happened. In point of fact, I wouldn't be at all surprised if Dennis had been the brains behind the name, now that I think about it, as he was terribly quick-thinking and witty back in the day and is responsible for combining my own names in a remarkably similar manner. My full name is Sally Amanda Smith. You can see, I imagine, why it might be that Dennis combined my names in jest one rainy afternoon sometime roundabout the early ninety-seventies, and refers to me often, and most affectionately, as Salamander instead. I don't mind it at all from Dennis, and Phyl has adopted it quite easily, but to most of Little Wittering I am known as Mrs Smith, as a result of my decades of authority in my position as a senior teacher in St Cuthbert's Secondary.

In point of fact, Dougal Rufus Finbury is also no longer a child, of course, but a man of approximately thirty years of age. Although Dennis assures me it is mere coincidence that the buffoon was amongst my final cohort of students before I took my retirement, I have fostered a long-held belief that if that year group had been a little less challenging, I may have held on for another year or so. Nonetheless, I must reassure you that I am quite the professional and I worked awfully hard to ensure I did not relay any personal preferences or dislikes of pupils in all my years as a teacher. Thus, you can be quite assured that I endeavoured to treat Dougal Rufus Finbury in a manner no different from any other student in my care. Nor, of course, however well it serves to describe the boy, do I refer to him as Doofus to anyone other than Dennis, who is well able to keep a confidence, and to Phyllis, as there are no secrets between us and we are terribly close. Whilst it must also be allowed that Finbury is no longer that rather irritating fifteen-year-old, although I envisage him as such, one must also suspect his appearance may have improved with time. His character, regrettably, has not.

"Oh bother," I said, under my breath. "We had better move quickly. Come along, Phyllis." With that, I nudged her towards the voice of the American and asked in a low voice whether there might be a chair I could avail of.

"April, isn't it?" Phyl said. "We've come to see how you are getting on. Have you made very much progress?"

I immediately gave my friend a little nudge. "Phyllis! We haven't time for pleasantries now. April, I must apologise for the intrusion, and it *had* quite been our intention to inquire as to your progress, and with a bit of my friend's Irish luck, we may still have such opportunity later. Meanwhile, as a matter of haste, would you be kind enough to tell us whether you remained at this computer station all morning?"

Phyllis nudged me onto a chair and I told Amity to sit beside me, which she did. She is very well-trained and even in the most unusual of circumstances, she is terribly obedient.

"May I pet her?" The American's voice was a little hesitant and just as I was about to explain about it, it wasn't at all necessary, as she carried on and said of course she realised she wasn't supposed to. "Not while she's in service. She's just so awfully cute, with those big deep eyes. I'm heartsick for my furbabies back home." She sounded terribly wistful and sad and I felt quite sorry for her being so far from home and uncertain as to the history of her past, and now caught up in all this kerfuffle in the library too.

I said of course I had never seen Amity's eyes or any other part of her for that matter, but I imagined them to be very wise and very soulful, as she is terribly good at being *my* eyes and looking after me. I relaxed the harness so April could give her a rub, and once that was done with, I said I expect she'd noticed, but the policeman who had just entered was quite the buffoon and Phyl and I had a notion about something and we wanted to find out about it before the policeman put his clumsy feet into it.

Of course, then we had to explain what we meant by buffoon, and then April agreed it did seem to be a suitable name to call him, and asked if our English policemen didn't wear those funny little helmets that looked like upside-down buckets, and Phyl said not very often. I had to hold up my hand as if I were teaching an unruly class of teenagers and say, "Ladies, we don't have much time so let's try to get to the point."

April gave a short laugh as if she were quite enthralled by the whole affair and said she had barely moved from this seat once she'd gotten some papers from the printer, except when she'd gotten up to ask about where to find a register. One of the librarians had directed her to the local history section and Phyl said, "Ooh, that's round about opposite the Cookery, so it's in the vicinity," and April said "Pardon?"

"Where poor Charlotte was taken ill," I said helpfully, as it seemed the poor woman was quite bewildered and not at all keeping up.

"And Charlotte is ...?"

"The head librarian."

"Darn. Is she going to be all right? But isn't that her over at the desk? She seems to be okay."

Phyl said no, that was Carrie, Charlotte was the one who'd been wheeled out on a stretcher, and Carrie wasn't the head even though she'd been the librarian for donkey's years, and April said that was another of our cute little British sayings and wasn't it wonderful. Phyl said that's all very well, but Carrie thought it *ought* to be her and she was quite put out that Charlotte had the promotion instead. April said that's a darn shame and didn't it explain her manner, and I said could she explain what she meant?

"When I asked the younger one about the records, she said I could use the microfiche and she was busy with something for a minute and she said the other one – her over there – would show me. The senior one wasn't at all happy about it and said something about how would she ever learn how to deal with it if she never did it. She looked right down her nose at me and said she supposed I'd never used one before either and she'd be over in a minute and she gave the young one such a look it would sour milk."

"And *did* Carrie come over and show you?"

"She went off to help him with something first, and then came over to me after that."

"Who do you mean by 'him'?"

"Ah, pardon me. I guess you can't see where I pointed. Him at that other computer. Big guy. Beard. Light-coloured hair."

"Gary?" Phyl said, so I supposed she was looking in whichever direction April gestured, and that Gary was still at the computer. April said, yes, that was him, and Phyl said, "She means Gary, Sally, he's still here. Sure, we'll be having a little chat with him next if I know anything about you, eh Sal?"

I gave her the smallest nod of my head to let her know she was perfectly accurate and I agreed wholeheartedly with her suggestion, but I had another question for April before we thought about chatting to Gary. "Where was Charlotte?"

"The younger librarian? She'd gone off with the man first after all, because the older one had to take a telephone call. She went after them once she was done, but I guess they didn't need her, because she came over to say she'd show me how to use the machine, not too long after. She took me off to the machine and told the other one to watch what we were doing. Said it was high time she learned how to use the thing because she wasn't going to be around forever to teach her how to do her job. The other one muttered something about the internet and digital files and the senior one said it would take years to get every old file digitised and for now, we were stuck with microfiche so she'd have to suck it up and learn it."

"Did you find what you were looking for?" Phyl asked. "Sure, if you are around town for a day or two, wouldn't I give you a hand with it, see if we can't find out something?"

"Phyllis was a librarian," I said. "She was terribly good at it and she is terribly nosey, too." Phyl batted me with her hand, although it is a perfectly accurate description and she couldn't possibly argue about the fact. "Did you overhear anything Gary might have said?" I didn't bother to add that I fully intended to pop over and ask him what he was looking for and whether Charlotte was acting at all oddly at that point in the morning, as I wanted to hear it from every angle, in case any of them had anything new to add to the mixture.

"I'd guess he was working on his resumé or something. He'd asked them if he could pop into that other room to spread out his papers and suchlike because the breeze was blowing them all over the place. It was kind of funny, that. They'd gone all over the floor multiple times by then. The younger one said just shut the window, but there was a bit of a protest about that. From him, too, as it was so hot. The uppity one – the older one, not the young one who's been taken away by the EMTs – said there were some items they'd need to move off the table. Then she said it needed tidying anyway so no time like the present. The younger one did go and see to it after all, because like I say, the senior one had to answer the telephone. I wasn't paying much attention, only that I was wating for someone to help me figure out what the micro machine gadget was, after they said to use it, and I needed assistance with it."

Phyllis chipped in to ask if by EMT, she was talking about our paramedics, and if I had the capability of giving her one of those daggery looks of Carrie's, I would have cast one towards her. She does have quite the tendency to go off tangent when something interesting catches her attention, which can be terribly infuriating when one is in a hurry.

"Did you see anyone else going off after Charlotte?" I said. "After she went with Gary? Did either of them appear to behave any differently after that?" It was most pertinent that we stay on track, as I was quite certain we would be interrupted just as soon as Finbury realised what we were up to. For once, I was grateful that he has such a predisposition to being slow off the mark and hadn't paid any attention to anyone besides Carrie, as far as I could tell from his voice and her increasingly irritated responses.

Before April could answer, Amity gave a low growl and got to her feet. Her harness shifted beneath my fingers and when

I placed a hand on her back, she was stiff and quivering, so I supposed immediately that I had somehow transported the thought into the buffoon's head and readied myself for the onslaught.

"Well, Ladies, what's going on here? Having a mothers' meeting are we, Mrs Smith?" The booming and obnoxious tones of Doofus Finbury penetrated our conversation, accompanied by the faint whiff of body odour and stale cigarettes and the squeak of over-shined shoes.

I gave an inward sigh. "Dougal Rufus. How lovely of you to come out so promptly to attend the scene." I managed to put as much of my sweet-old-lady into my voice as is possible when one is resisting the urge to vomit on a man's shoes. "Have you made an arrest yet?"

He gave a rather unpleasant snort and said that not every death in a public location was suspicious and some people died of natural causes.

I retorted in my most pleasant manner that I was not unaccustomed to death from natural causes, and had attended quite the number of funerals thank you very much. "However," I said sweetly, "on this particular occasion, Police Constable Finbury, I would suggest very strongly that you examine the evidence and address this as a suspicious incident. Of course, if you are so inclined to dismiss my suggestions as those of a batty old woman, I am sure your supervisor will have no great sorrow in reprimanding you."

"You might even lose your shiny little Sheriff badge," Phyl said. I was terribly worried I may giggle at that, as Phyl and I have an ongoing joke about how we always imagine Doofus to be wearing one of those little toy badges pinned to his puffed-out chest in a most prominent position. Dennis and Frederick say we are terribly childish about it, but I think you will agree there is much to be said for finding something amusing in even the most unsavoury of situations.

Finbury emitted a rather unpleasant harrumph.

I caught a distinct whiff of bacon so it was quite clear he had indulged in a bacon sandwich. I supposed he'd been into one of the cafés for his breakfast – the Bread and Breakfast if I'm not mistaken, as they are more inclined to do that sort of thing – and that was what had prevented him from arriving before poor Charlotte's body was wheeled off on the stretcher. I must say I thought this was quite the example of the kind of shoddy policework one gets complaints about in the Guardian, and I said as much to him.

He blustered in that ridiculous manner of his, but he didn't deny it so I supposed I was quite correct. Then he said if we had nothing better to do than sit around gossiping, he would be most obliged if we stopped it at once so as not to hinder his investigations.

It was Phyl's turn to give quite the snort. When she had recovered herself by pretending she had a tickle in her throat, she said hadn't he just said it wasn't at all suspicious so was he investigating a suspicious death or wasn't he?

I had another little inward chuckle at that. Phyllis is terribly sharp when she wants to be and she had a perfectly good point.

"You might find it useful to make up your mind about it," she said, which I must say I thought was most amusing of her, although I couldn't imagine at all what April must be thinking and wondered if she might think us awfully rude to be heckling with an officer of the law, but of course she hadn't the experience of Doofus Finbury that Phyl and I have. I hoped at that moment that Phyllis and April *would* get a chance to meet up, if only so Phyllis could demonstrate that we are not at all unkind as a matter of course. Dennis does remind us from time to time that Doofus Finbury really does bring out the worst in us, and I do concede the point. Dougal Finbury brings out the worst in most people, if one is perfectly frank.

Nevertheless, I decided I should rise above my personal feeling for the incompetent Finbury and said in as level and pleasant voice as I could muster, "April here is visiting from the States. She was just telling us that she didn't see Charlotte after she went off into the meeting room with Gary here, although several other people came and went, so perhaps that will give you something to start from."

"Right. You. Come with me. We shall command a room and I shall conduct some interviews."

I was quite certain he meant he might commandeer a room, but I expect he might not know a word of so many syllables, but I kept the thought to myself as I had a more pertinent point to clarify: "To whom are you speaking? If you are waving that pointy little finger of yours in my direction, I must remind you I am quite unable to see it."

"I shall speak to this woman here. Avril, you can come with me. And I will thank you two – yes, that includes you, Mrs Smith – I will thank you to wait quietly until such time as I require you to give a statement, although I imagine it won't be necessary. I suggest you go off and read some books about knitting or whatever it is you do now you have retired."

"I will remind you, Dougal Finbury, that I am no longer able to read, and I would expect that even a person who has scraped through Police Training with the barest of ability would be able to deduce that a blind woman is unlikely to read a knitting pattern, wouldn't you agree?"

He stammered a bit at that and Phyllis told me afterwards that he had turned a rather unbecoming shade of red. Off he squeaked, with the American woman in tow, leaving Phyl and I free to have a little chat with the two men in the computer section, so it seemed apparent that he hadn't thought that through at all as I was quite sure he wouldn't approve of us having any kind of conversation with the witnesses at all, however innocent it may be. Especially not one who was also a most likely suspect in the case.

Chapter Seven

It seemed sensible to start with Gary, as I knew him already and had never met the other one – the man the ladies had described in varying degrees of compliments from 'lush' to 'delicious' to 'very handsome' and a particularly lewd comment from Joan, which was perfectly inappropriate yet had caused quite the chuckle around the table and I had very much wished I was able to see him for myself.

I got to my feet and asked Amity to take me to speak with Gary, but as she doesn't know Gary at all, she didn't entirely understand the command and wasn't at all sure in which direction she should lead me. I called out, "Excuse me, is Gary here somewhere?" and two people answered at once.

"'ere."

"There."

I pricked my ears to ascertain the direction in which I needed to set foot, and a voice I presumed to be Gary's said, "I'm at the next computer. Just 'ere. If you turn a little to your left, then about four steps ..." and then Phyl said, "Over here," and took me by the arm and all but dragged me the predicted four steps at which location someone said, "'ere's a chair, Mrs Smith." There was the *ssh*ing sound of a chair pulled across that kind of short rough carpet one expects in a library if a softer acoustic has been agreed upon, and I patted the air until I made contact with the plastic shape of yet another of those stackable types of chair upon which one does not like to remain seated for very long.

"Goodness. Are all the chairs at the computers of this type? I shouldn't think that encourages anyone to get very much done." Nonetheless, I sat upon the blessed thing, as one does tend to find it is easier to be seated when one cannot see one's surroundings beyond the very foggiest of light and shadow. "Have *you* made much progress in your endeavours today?" I asked Gary.

He said he had made a little, thank you very much, and he had an interview lined up for that afternoon, so he'd nipped along to the library to brush up on the company. I asked what was the company, and it turned out to be one of those places that sells electrical contraptions such as toasters and vacuum cleaners. I believe Gary must be quite skilled in that sort of thing, as Dennis had been tackling the lawn mower on the day Gary had popped round to paint our fence and between the pair of them, they'd got it working again. I expect you will have guessed that had been the end of my peaceful afternoon listening to a book in the garden, as Dennis had immediately decided to mow the lawn while he had the machine going.

"This nice American woman said she'd seen you nipping off somewhere with Charlotte," I said, and he said it was a terrible business and he had hoped she would be okay but it seemed rather unlikely as she had looked awfully pale as they whisked her out. Phyl said she appeared to be dead, and Gary said, yes, he thought that might be the case but he hadn't liked to say so in case we hadn't heard.

"How was she when you spoke to her? Did she appear to be ill?"

"Came with me int' meeting room," he said. "Cleared some space a' table for me t' spread ou' paperwork. Bit grudging, she were, never keenest t' lift a finger, 'er." He stopped abruptly as if realising he was speaking ill of the dead. "Oh. Bit o' shock, in't it. Don' expect a dead 'un on your 'ands in library an' all."

"On your hands?" I said, as I must say it seemed an odd choice of words and I wondered if there wasn't a little clue in that.

"Manner o' speaking. She weren't dead when I left 'er, Mrs Smith, tha' she were'n'."

I wondered for a moment if he might be telling me he had left her in such a state that he knew her death to be imminent, but Gary is a perfectly pleasant and helpful man so I brushed away the thought at once. I simply couldn't fathom any plausible likelihood that he had done anything to her, so I supposed he hadn't meant that at all. Moreover, even though Gary had readily admitted to being alone in the meeting room with poor Charlotte, it, like that utilised by the book club ladies, was open to the main library as far as I could tell. Anyone with the benefit of eyesight might have been able to see what was going on therein, so it seemed most unlikely anyone would choose such a location to brutally kill someone, don't you think?

This thought was proven to be accurate not a minute later, as Finbury's voice called across the library: "You there, close this door. We shall need privacy."

It was entirely unclear to whom he addressed the order, but Phyllis mumbled, "Poor Carrie," in a most sympathetic tone, so I deduced it was her, and I was proved right immediately when Carrie answered the unpleasant little flibbert.

"You mean the sliding wall," she said, her voice laced with sarcasm. "I will do that for you at once, Constable Finbury. All you need to do is pull it, but perhaps it was too complicated for you." There followed the ungainly sound of the corrugated divider being dragged across the opening, and Carrie muttering in a terribly cross tone about the little good it would do him.

So you can see, the sliding wall must have been open all along until that point, as there had been none of the noise of it being moved during the morning. One does tend to hear any kind of noise, when one is in a library, however much one tries to filter it out.

Regardless of whether the divider had been open or closed, or whether one could see in or not, I felt it most unlikely that Gary had killed Charlotte in the meeting room, as Phyllis had been quite certain that poor Charlotte had been found amongst the Cookery books, in the non-fiction section of the library. I imagine that even a blind woman might have noticed the kerfuffle of a person dragging a corpse across the room from one place to another, even if parts of the floor were covered in hard-wearing industrial carpet and other parts floored with that artificial wooden whatnot. Nonetheless, I suppose one could check whether there were any signs of scuffle or smears of blood, and I made a mental note to ask Phyllis to take a look at the areas in question, and then a realisation came upon me and I said, "*Was* there very much blood?" as no one had made any kind of reference to such a thing.

Gary said he'd been there, and hadn't noticed any blood. Well, that jangled another small bell of alarm, and I had a most unpleasant notion that perhaps there was something in the fact he had now told us twice that he had been with Charlotte around the time of her death. Of course, it was also most likely, given the proximity of both the meeting room and the computer section to the non-fiction section – which is placed between the two – that he had merely been the first to respond to a cry for help. I supposed anyone arriving upon the scene would have been able to observe whether or not there was a vast pool of blood around the victim. Phyl must have read my mind, as she so often does, because she said she hadn't thought there could have been much blood about the place.

"No one said anything about it," she said. "Sure, wouldn't one have expected to hear some kind of squeal or shout if it was that kind of injury?"

I had a bit of a think and tried to imagine the scenario in my mind, and concluded I had to agree with her about the squeal of pain if one was killed in such a manner as to bleed on the library floor. I told Phyl she was probably right about that, and perhaps Ashwini might be able to enlighten us on the matter, and she and Gary and I fell into a little silence. I supposed the three of us were taking a moment to consider the unpleasantness of someone being fiendishly killed in such a peaceful and unassuming location as the non-fiction section of the Little Wittering Library.

From the desk area there came the low rumble of quietly-speaking voices, although the sound was almost drowned out by Finbury's clumsy attempts to interrogate the poor American woman, booming out from beyond the newly-closed corrugated wall. I supposed Josephine had made Carrie that cup of tea and thought I might pop over and see if there was enough left in the kettle for Phyl and I to partake in a cup too. Just as I was thinking about suggesting it to Phyllis, my thoughts were interrupted by the kind of sniffing one associates with a bout of hayfever, or a person who is in some distress, yet wishes to conceal the fact.

"Phyl," I said in my quietest whisper, "Won't you look around in a most discreet kind of a way and see if someone in the vicinity is having a bit of a cry?"

Gary must have overheard, because he said in a low voice that it looked like the young fellow at the other computer was, and I said did he mean the good-looking one all the Book Club ladies had been raving about?

"'ow would I know?" Gary said with a bit of a chuckle. "Can't say as I'd fancy 'im meself." Then he informed me that the fellow was facing away from us anyway, as that computer faced the wall dividing the computers from the books, but then he must have given it a bit of consideration because he added, "Reckon me wife would, if I still 'ad one." He gave a bitter kind of a laugh as if there were nothing amusing about it at all, so I supposed it might have been a fairly recent development.

I was most taken aback, as I hadn't been aware that Gary's marriage had been in any kind of upheaval, but Gary is not a person with whom I am closely acquainted, so I suppose I might not have heard about it.

"I'm sorry to hear that," I said, although he may have imagined I was referring to the man sobbing sniffily somewhere nearby, as he said, "'ee's in a right two an' eight. 'ad quite the thing for 'er, been following 'er around for weeks. Like a wet dog, 'ee is."

I didn't see the connection about being a wet dog, as Amity prefers to go off and have a bit of shake when she has been caught in the rain, rather than follow anyone anywhere, but I am quite *au fait* with rhyming slang. Dennis used to be a milkman and he had a colleague in the dairy who was one of those proper Londoners, from under the Bow bells or somewhere thereabouts. Dennis had quite the fascination for that kind of thing and we had a great deal of fun practising it in the evenings, like a little code between us, so I knew at once that Gary meant the other man was in a bit of state. Of course, I wondered at once what exactly it was that had the other man in such a state, so you won't be at all surprised that I accepted Gary's invitation, even though I was perfectly certain it was a figure of speech and not intended to encourage further interrogation. "I *will* ask you, since you have suggested it. By *he*, I presume you mean the young man called Harry?"

"Yeah, 'arry. Tha's righ'."

"Why do you suppose he is quite so distressed? Was he close to Charlotte?"

"Well, quite the shock, ay?" Gary paused for a moment and I supposed he might be thinking about what a shock it had been to him, too, so I said, "Yes, I'm quite sure it must have been a terrible surprise for everyone, but no one else is sobbing into their computer about it, as far as I can tell."

Gary agreed about that, and said perhaps Harry was more upset because he'd known her quite well. I was momentarily glad for all the sniffing and low sobbing, as although it made it a little more difficult for me to hear what Gary had to say about it, I hoped that Harry might not realise we were speaking about him. One never likes to be thought of a gossip, I'm sure you agree?

"Infatuated with 'er, always 'anging around 'er like a bad smell. Right fed up with 'im, she were." I was most relieved that Gary dwelt a little less upon the young man's looks than had our Book Club ladies, as there is only so much usefulness in describing a person's looks as opposed to their behaviour when one is trying to fathom out a murder mystery. Gary, fortunately, was most forthcoming about the behaviour side of things, and told me in quite some detail how he had observed, throughout that morning, and other mornings previously, that Harry had appeared to not utilise the computer at which he sat. He was, apparently, entirely smitten with poor Charlotte and appeared to pass his time gazing dreamily after the young librarian, wherever she walked and whatever she appeared to be doing.

"Now an' then 'ee'd get up an' talk to 'er, follow 'er off int' the books or … Been at it for weeks. Like I say, 'ee's quite a thing for 'er. Smitten."

"And was it reciprocated?" I asked, even though I had been unwittingly party to Charlotte's own opinion on the matter and was, therefore, quite aware of the answer.

"Recipowhat? Did she fancy 'im too, you mean? Shoul'nt say so," Gary said, without so much as a pause to consider the matter. "Shot 'im daggers, she did, when she caught 'im at it.

Take s'morning, fr'instance – she came over not long after 'ee got 'ere. Asked 'im t' leave."

"And he said?"

"'Ah, don't be like that, Charl,' 'ee said. Knew she were finding it 'ard, settling in an' all that. Keeping an eye, 'ee said 'ee were."

"What did she say to that?"

"Said she were fine, an' 'ee really oughta go. Then 'ee said 'ee weren't doing no 'arm an' 'ad as much right t' be 'ere as anyone. Might do a bit o' research, 'ee said, but I could see there weren't nothing on 'is screen. Can see the screens from 'ere. The one 'ee's using faces one way away from me and the one the woman's using faces the other. 'ers is in front o' window, like. Mine faces the wall."

I find it terribly encouraging when a person takes time to describe things to me, and it rather proves my point about Gary being perfectly pleasant and helpful, so you can see how I couldn't think it could have been him, even after he said he'd been off in the meeting room with Charlotte.

"Funny how they've put 'em like it," he went on. "You'd think they'd give some privacy but if they were other way round with our backs t' the wall and the computer screens facing outwards, it'd be better, woul'nt it? Anyway, yeah, 'ee weren' doing nowt much with it. You know 'ow they go all blank when you ain't pressed anything for a while?"

That sounded a lot like my eyesight, now I think about it, so I could imagine it quite well when he described it, although it's been a terribly long time since I saw such a thing. Nowadays, of course, I rely solely on the clever little speaking application on the rare occasions I need to avail of a computer, which is not often at all. Even with the voice recognition contraption, I must admit I find it terribly difficult to navigate any kind of computer, and Dennis isn't much better even though he can see perfectly well. Nevertheless, it appeared to be a rhetorical question, so I didn't bother to explain. "Go on," I said instead, so he did.

"She clearly were'n 'appy, but off she went. Saw 'er talking t' the other one 'bout it – Carrie – and she gave 'im a bit of an eye but din't say nothing. She din't like Charlotte much, can tell that a'right. Much as 'ee watched 'er like a lovesick puppy, Carrie'd look at 'er like she'd kill – oh!" He gave a deep little gasp and there was the faintest slap as if he'd clapped a hand to his mouth upon realising what he had just said.

"She *detested* her. That's why I weren't going nowhere." The voice was not Gary's. It was most indignant and came from somewhere behind me, and to the left of where we sat at Gary's computer station, so I guessed at once it must be the allegedly delectable Harry. Even without the clue of the man's proximity, the only other man within the library besides Gary and he, so far as I could tell, was Police Constable Doofus Finbury, and I'd know his voice anywhere.

Even at that moment, the little gimlet's voice was bouncing around my eardrums. It was only by some small miracle that the incompetent's voice was not drowning out every other sound in the library and that I could discern any level of conversation with the other customers. Fortunately, I had developed quite the aptitude for blocking him out during several entirely unpleasant terms of practice in the classroom some fifteen years before, or thereabouts, when I had the misfortune to be the boy's form tutor in 5S.

I turned a little in my seat in order that I may address Harry directly, and asked him if he wouldn't mind explaining exactly what he meant by saying Charlotte had detested Carrie.

"No, it were the other way around. Charlie weren't like that. She liked everyone. Carrie hated *Charlie*. Anyone could tell. Ever since Charl' got promoted. Charl' *deserved* the promotion. She'd trained for it and gone to university for it and everything. That's why she was brought in for it. Old bat should be retired. Charl' said so, too."

"She did?" I was quite surprised to hear this, although it perfectly reiterated Phyllis's observations, so I supposed she was onto something when she'd said there was no love lost between the librarians. I suppose it just goes to show what kind of visual clues one may miss if one is unable to observe a person's facial expressions. "I was under the impression that they were perfectly pleasant and amicable in their conversations with one another. I've quite had my eyes opened about it, in a manner of speaking. Goodness."

"I did tell you so," said Phyllis, and I must say she sounded terribly smug about it, as she does like to be right about things.

"You did," I agreed, and she didn't say anything, so I'm sure she realised at once that I was distracted by the matter, as I would not usually be so quick to give her the satisfaction. Even though I am the kind of person who will readily admit when I have made a mistake, Phyllis and I do have that kind of rivalry one finds among those who have been friends for over forty years, in which each of us takes a certain satisfaction in ousting the other whenever we get the chance.

"Would you mind telling me what you think might have happened to poor Charlotte?" I rather thought that by putting on my sweet-old-lady voice, Harry would be more inclined to indulge me than had I approached the matter in my teacher's voice. "I find it terribly confusing that a person has been murdered in the library and I have no way to see what is happening about the place." I added a little shudder, for emphasis, and it seemed to work as he was quite forthcoming when he spoke about it, albeit a little broken up by sniffs and gulps.

Charlotte was his girlfriend, he said, so he liked to pop in and be with her when he could, to keep an eye on things, especially since she'd said Carrie was unhappy about not getting the promotion.

I didn't say anything to suggest that I had overheard quite the evidence that Charlotte had certainly *not* considered herself to be his girlfriend, at least, not anymore. I wasn't at all inclined to let something slip that might start him off again, not when he'd finally stopped sniffling, which was quite the blessing. Besides, just at that moment, another thought had occurred to me about something Phyllis had said when she was peering under the bookshelves to find out what might be going on, and I wondered if he might say something about that if he kept talking. However, I kept that thought to myself for the moment and selected a question to which I suspected he may be more forthcoming in his answer.

"Why didn't you go with her? In the ambulance?"

He made a few of those funny little sounds one makes when one is thinking about how to answer a difficult question, or when one is caught in a trap. I imagined he might be opening and closing his mouth in the manner of a fish, but then he said, "I suppose it was all a bit of a shock, and I didn't think they'd let me," which was a perfectly reasonable answer, if one thinks about it.

"Not because you aren't together anymore, so?"

I patted around to find where Phyllis was standing behind me, and found her hand resting on the back of my chair. I gave her a little pat, and I'm sure she realised what I meant, as she continued with that line of questioning.

"I was sure she said you'd split up, quite some weeks ago … sure, I could be mistaken, so."

I'm quite sure you will be familiar with those wonderful Good Cop, Bad Cop routines in those evening dramas that have become so popular nowadays. Dennis and I do enjoy them, and endeavour to put them on whenever Dennis notices one is scheduled while he is looking through the *TV Times*. Of course, he can see quite clearly what is unfolding on the screen whereas I must pay good attention to the audible clues, but between us, we are terribly accurate in working it out. Phyllis, it must be said, is wonderfully adept at playing the Bad Cop when the need arises, and now I come to think of it, we got out of many a scrape in our teacher-training days in exactly this manner.

"No, I'm quite sure she said you'd broken up." Phyllis said again, as if she'd given it quite the thought. She was quite matter of fact and blunt about it, and the young man gave a sharp intake of breath as if this might be the first time he'd heard such a thing, which goes to show how deluded he seemed to be about the situation. All at once, I understood exactly what it was Gary had meant about the fellow gazing wistfully at the young librarian instead of doing anything at all useful or productive while he sat at the computer. I may not be able to see it for myself, but it is perfectly easy to imagine a lovesick young man behaving in just such a way, especially when one has experiences of teaching class after class of hormone-laden adolescents.

At Phyllis's comment, the sniffing took up once more. After a moment or two of that, there came an altogether louder sniff muffled by something that one might hope to be a handkerchief but I imagine was most likely to be a sleeve or suchlike.

"We were on a break." He said it awfully quietly, and only that I was concentrating hard on eliminating the hoohah coming from the meeting room where Finbury was, no doubt, being terribly intimidating in his manner towards the poor American visitor, was I able to discern Harry's words.

"Am I to presume that 'on a break' means you felt you were, in fact, still a couple?" I asked gently. "Is that why you referred to her as your girlfriend?"

He sniffed again. "She is – was – my girlfriend. We were going to get *married*." He sounded quite mutinous about it, as if it were decided, and the mere fact of Charlotte's lack of interest in the matter was entirely irrelevant.

"Mate," Gary said, "You really weren'. Anyone'd see she weren' int' you. She ask'd you t' leave 'er alone. An' it weren' the firs' time, were it?"

"She didn't mean it. We was working it out."

"Mate." Although I couldn't be sure what he looked like, besides large and bearded, I imagined him to have an expression of sympathy about his face, as his tone was remarkably gentle. "You need t' leave 'er alone – oh. Er ... Well."

A heavy, warbling sigh came from my left, then tremored into a series of rapid gasps until another sob broke free.

"You could 'ave anyone, mate. That young black girl's a pretty wee thing, an' 'as all puppy dog eyes on you an' you din't even give 'er a glance when she were over 'ere trying t' get your attention. I'd say you oughtta forget about Charlotte, only 'sa bit late for tha', in't it." Gary broke off abruptly, then uttered a profanity I don't care to repeat, and there was a *pfft*, a shift in the air, and a movement of shadow the size of a large man, and a bit of a shuffle. "Ge' a grip, mate, ge' a grip." Gary's voice became muffled and faint and there followed a series of sniffs and the sound one might associate with one person slapping another on the shoulder a few times. I wondered if Gary might be giving the younger man one of those man-hugs Dennis occasionally talks about being popular amongst the younger generation. If I was at all correct about that, it would certainly prove me to be also correct in my impression that Gary really is a terribly pleasant man, wouldn't you agree?

The bulky shadow shifted past me again and there was the soft *whssh* one might presume to be a man setting his weight fully onto a plastic library chair.

"Now. Ge' yourself together and you oughtta tell Mrs Smith 'ere 'bout 'ow you 'ad your lovely Charlotte cornered, ay?" Gary's voice was altogether firmer and had quite lost the sympathetic manner of a few moments previously, which left me quite bewildered about it and not at all certain of his character after all.

The sniffling and sobbing ceased abruptly. "What do you mean?" Harry's voice became rather pitched, and held quite the tone of indignant surprise.

"Over there."

"He's pointing at the wall, so I think he means in the non-fic, behind it," Phyllis whispered helpfully.

"When I were comin' out the meeting room, after she'd lef' me t' ge' on with it, you and 'er were in a' the back there. 'ad yer back t' me, you did, an' she was in with 'er back up agains' the books an' coul'nt ge' pas' you. Dunno what you was saying t' each other, jus' lef' you to it, din't I? Shoulda intervened, ay? Only tha' girl came up, an' I reckoned she were going t' say something, so I lef' you t' it."

Phyllis gave a little gasp, and I quite agreed with her, as it was quite the surprise to hear there had been such an obvious altercation. One would think such a confrontation as Gary described would have made quite the noise, but I suppose one can argue perfectly quietly if one is in a public location, as Dennis and I managed to do after he mistakenly ordered me liver although I had clearly asked him to order me the calamari when we were in Devon on holiday some years ago. How one can be married for so many years and still unaware of one's wife's dislike of offal, one simply cannot fathom.

However, before I had the opportunity to digest this important piece of evidence, there was the unpleasant interruption of Doofus Finbury, who announced quite loudly and clearly that he was done with speaking to the American woman. "Would the man in the cap proceed to the meeting room to be interviewed?" he said, in those pompous tones he is inclined to adopt whenever he utilises a phrase clearly taught to him in police training college, but of which I suspect he retained no comprehension at all.

"Which of you is wearing a cap?" I said.

"Me."

"'im."

I deduced from their overlapping responses that it was Harry to whom Finbury addressed his command, and I wondered why it might be that Finbury had chosen that order of proceedings, and whether April might have said something to have led Finbury to imagine Harry was, indeed, responsible for Charlotte's demise. Of course, you will agree from the account of his behaviour how this may be a perfectly logical conclusion, and might understand why Finbury would think such a thing. Nonetheless, I was yet to be convinced. There were still several pieces of the puzzle to put into place and one could simply not ignore Isobel's suspicious activity, and it was that, I decided, that I should try to get to the bottom of at once.

Chapter Eight

Harry gave another of his sniffles and Phyllis said, "For goodness' sake get yourself a tissue on the way and pull yourself together or he'll have you locked up before you say another word. Here." There was a bit of ruffling and rummaging and it was only then that I realised dear Phyllis had carried her handbag with her across the room.

I had left mine on the table in the meeting room as it really is quite enough to manage Amity's harness and Phyllis's arm, without the all kerfuffle of a handbag, and if anyone felt so inclined to steal it they would be terribly disappointed to find little more than a large and specially-adapted mobile telephone that offers none of the nifty modern applications one expects from an iPhone 47 or whatever number of the blessed things the Apple people are onto these days; a packet of those handy pocket tissues; a tube of Polo mints; a dog lead, and a handful of dog treats. Not even a key to my house, as Dennis is home and will greet me at the door. He has an uncanny ability to sense my arrival, much as one expects from a pet dog, and will without fail be awaiting me on the doorstep with a, "There you are then, safely home, my clever little Salamander," and a peck on the cheek. He really is quite a dear, if one overlooks the little irritations one must expect when one has been married for such a long time.

I'm afraid I have digressed a little, which just goes to show how much of a distraction Doofus Finbury can be.

Gary didn't seem to have much more to add to the conversation, once Harry had been taken off by Finbury, and I was certain that Phyllis would be rather hoping for that cup of tea by that point. Therefore, although it had been terribly interesting to hear what Gary and April and Harry all had to say for themselves, I couldn't help but wonder if I may glean something just as helpful from another means, particularly when one considers that I had collected up quite a few leads by then. Most pressing in my mind was a keen desire to find out exactly what it was that Isobel had been up to.

Leaving Phyllis and I free to confer with the others was not the only thing Doofus Finbury had overlooked when he had commandeered the right-hand meeting room. As I think I have mentioned, I am entirely perplexed as to how one so incompetent could possibly have passed through the police training examinations or whatnot, and I particularly fail to understand why he appears not to have been instructed in the nature of discretion. Police Constable Finbury has a voice, you see, that *carries*. You will also recall that even though the little gimlet had somehow had the idea, if not the ability, of pulling across the concertina-type room divider, it was not an adequate barrier to sound. Thus, even the most unobservant amongst us would have found it difficult to ignore the conversation emitting from the meeting room. And I, with my finely attuned sense of hearing, could hear every word uttered by the incompetent fool.

Nonetheless, it can be challenging to give one's full attention to several conversations simultaneously, so I said to Gary perhaps he would be kind enough to ensure the American had not been too perturbed by her encounter with Constable Finbury, but I needed to pop to the lavatory so I would leave them to it. I said to Phyllis that if she didn't mind, she might be kind enough to accompany me, in case Amity became at all confused by all the unexpected comings and goings.

Of course, Phyllis is perfectly aware that I need no such help, and that Amity is entirely trustworthy and capable, but she guessed immediately that I had something up my sleeve so she helped me to my feet and said, "Are you okay, dear?"

I was quite certain it was not me to whom she was speaking, as she has never referred to me as 'dear' in all the years we have known each other. Sure enough, it was the American who answered and said, yes, thank you, she was fine.

"I say," she said, after the briefest of pauses, "are *all* your policemen like that? He's not like our policemen home in the States, you know?"

I must say she sounded quite bewildered by the experience. I was not at all surprised about it, of course, as that is the effect P.C. Finbury has on a person, I'm afraid.

Phyllis must have had the same thought, about how April must be getting quite the bad impression of Little Wittering by now, because she said, "You sit here with Gary and I'll see if someone might get you a nice cup of tea."

Off went Phyllis and I, in the direction of the lavatories, via the desk, where I suggested someone, Josephine, perhaps, as she is terribly good at that sort of thing, might offer refreshments to our American visitor.

"Perhaps you'd pop enough water in the kettle for Phyllis and me, too," I added hopefully.

Josephine said she was about to refill it anyway, because there'd only been enough for Carrie and Ashwini and Barbara and Joan and herself in the first lot, once Finbury had procured a cup for himself.

I'd quite forgotten about poor Ashwini again, as she is a quiet sort of person and hadn't been with us in the book club meeting for very long that morning before all the hoohah had erupted with Charlotte. "Goodness, Ashwini, it's terribly lucky you were here this morning."

"There wasn't much I could do," she said, and I readjusted my angle as I had been facing in quite the wrong direction. "The poor girl was dead. Carrie has had a terrible shock. I imagine we'll be able to go soon, once that policeman has finished up, and she can close the library for the day and get herself home."

"Was she already dead when you got to her?" I asked, and Ashwini said yes, that had appeared to be the case, and it must have been something very sudden, for her to have just collapsed like that without making any sound.

"Was there an injury?" I asked.

Ashwini said, no, there didn't appear to be anything obvious, and she really couldn't say what have might been the cause, although if Dr Patil were present, no doubt he'd have known at once. She holds her husband in the highest esteem, although I wondered if it might be a little misplaced in this instance, as one would imagine it might not be obvious at all if there were no gaping shotgun wound or blood-stained knife sticking from a chest or whatnot.

"Was there anything at all odd about the situation?"

"Except for her being dead," Phylis added helpfully.

Ashwini had a little think and said she really didn't know, as she'd been too busy worrying about first aid and whether to call her husband or an ambulance, and then someone had taken the dilemma out of her hands and called an ambulance anyway, but by then, they were all quite certain it would be too late to save Charlotte, and wasn't it a shame as she was so young.

I wasn't entirely sure of the logic in that as I thought it a shame to murder anyone, whatever age the victim might be, but I suppose she wasn't thinking clearly and I was glad that Josephine had shown the sense to get her a cup of tea. "Who was nearby?" I said, as what I had remembered whilst Phyllis and I were speaking with the distraught young Harry, was that Phyl had been quite certain there had been three or four pairs of shoes visible to her beneath the bookshelves, not counting Charlotte's. I very much wanted to be sure as to whom the shoes belonged, in case it was important to the case.

Ashwini didn't say anything for a moment or two, so I imagine she was getting it clearer in her own mind before she spoke. "The two men. Carrie. I think only those."

"Were they present already, or did they arrive after you?"

There was another brief pause over which Finbury's bombastic tones could be clearly heard, asking Harry the most inane kinds of questions, such as whether he was known to the deceased, which anyone could have already discerned by that point, and whether he had moved the body. That, of course, was something *anybody* would be unlikely to admit to, had they done so. Whatever Harry said in reply was quite inaudible, as Finbury barely gave him a chance to respond before barking the next inopportune question.

"They were there already, I think," Ashwini said in her careful manner. "I can't be absolutely sure, but I think they were, because one of them was sitting on one of those step things with his head in his hands. I had to ask him to move a little so I could get to Charlotte's airways, but then I worried he might be about to faint so I told him to stay still and moved around him."

"One of those step things?"

"Like they stand on to reach the high-up books," Josephine said. "Is that what you mean, Ashwini?"

"One of those roundy-type step-stool yokes you can scoot around the floor on," Phyl added helpfully.

Of course, once Phyllis described it, I could perfectly imagine it, and an unwarranted image of my dear friend scooting around the place on such a contraption popped into my mind, and I'm sorry to admit I almost gave a little giggle at the thought. Then I was struck immediately by another, altogether more serious notion, which took the humour right out of the image. "Might Charlotte have fallen off it? Was it terribly high?"

"Only a foot or so off the ground, Sal, you know the sort." Phyllis would know about that kind of thing as she would have hopped on and off them quite frequently in her time, although I doubt she'd manage it now.

"I suppose it's possible," Ashwini said slowly. "But ..."

"Wouldn't someone have heard? Surely she'd have squealed?" I don't think I'd realised that Barbara was still at the desk until she spoke, but I appreciated her calm analysis of the situation and must say I was inclined to agree with her. One simply can't imagine a person falling silently, even if they are accustomed to working in the hushed environment of the Little Wittering Library. One would expect the surprise of it to cause at least a small shriek, not to mention the impact as one hits the ground, which, you will agree, would certainly incur some kind of thump, however plush the carpet may be. I think I have mentioned that the carpet in the library is *not* of the plush kind. Besides, I don't believe it covers the floor in the area in which Charlotte appears to have lain, if my memory is correct. Although, I suppose, if one thinks about, people must drop books on the library floor from time to time, so perhaps it is not entirely surprising that none of us seemed to have noticed any kind of thumping sound, and it were nothing unusual at all.

"Remind me," I said, addressing no one in particular, as it hardly seemed to matter whom amongst us may provide the answer, "is that section carpeted, or is it the laminate whatnot that we are currently standing on?"

It was quickly confirmed that the entire main room is floored in the same laminate, and only the children's area, the computer area, and the two meeting rooms are carpeted.

"For easier cleaning and heavier footfall," Carrie said with the weight of resignation in her words. "I don't see it makes any difference, and as no one eats or drinks in the main part, there's a lot more gets spilled on the carpets, if you ask me. Especially in Children's."

"Would you think she'd have looked more awkward?" Ashwini said. "If she'd fallen." Of course, none of us other than Carrie were in any kind of position to remark on this, so we were none the wiser, although after a moment, Carrie did say she really couldn't see how anyone could fall off such a low stool and knock themselves out so thoroughly as to kill themselves, whilst neither calling out for help nor leaving a vast puddle of blood in their wake.

"I do agree," Ashwini said, and sighed quite heavily, which caused Amity to thump her tail against my leg in sympathy.

"Was there anything else of note?"

"Or just a note," Barbara said, and although her tone remained as flat and dry as ever, that and my thinking about the thumping noises gave me another little idea.

"Or any books? If she had been climbing on the step, one might imagine she was either shelving or retrieving a book, don't you agree? Would anyone happen to know whether there were any books on the floor where Charlotte was found? Perhaps someone might like to have a quick look?" I was rather hopeful someone might pop over and assess the scene of the crime before Finbury got the idea from someone and barged in on his squeaky shoes and trampled over any evidence.

Phyllis must have been quite tuned in to my train of thought, as she often is, because she said, "Oh, yes, good idea, Sally!" and sounded terribly excited that we might get some ideas before the police found them. It goes without saying that neither Phyl nor I are the type of person to *interfere* or to hinder a police investigation. Nevertheless, when one has had the misfortune of teaching Dougal Finbury during his younger years, one could be entirely confident he was most predisposed to make quite the botch of it all. Thus, it seemed entirely pertinent to make our own observations of the situation, in order to assist with inquiries once someone efficient and capable arrived to sort it all out, as they would undoubtedly need to do.

I'm sure by now you have deduced that I was tuning in and out of the many separate conversations taking place around me, much as one does when one is listening to something interesting on the radio at the same time as one is having a conversation with someone who has called to one's doorstop in an attempt to sell something. Every now and then, therefore, I would allow my ear to tune in to what Finbury was saying to Harry, whom he still held captive in the meeting room. As Finbury was largely barking orders and accusations and allowing little opportunity for Harry to reply, I gleaned little from either one, and quickly reverted my attention to the conversation with Ashwini and Carrie and the other ladies from the book group until the next moment I might catch a glimmer of something pertinent emanating from the right-hand meeting room. Once one has learned to become largely reliant on one's hearing to compensate for losing one's eyesight, it becomes remarkably easy, over time, to filter the background noises from the important noises, and it was entirely in this manner of filtering the sounds that another useful snippet made itself known.

"Well –" Harry's voice rose indignantly above that of Doofus, and I was fleetingly amused at the similarities in the whining tones of the two men behind the corrugated room divider. "That Gary geezer didn't like her a bit, so maybe you should get him in here and point your fat finger at him instead."

Well, I pricked my ears up at that, let me tell you, as I had not been aware of any disagreements between Gary and Charlotte, and Gary had given us no clues to any such conflict. As I had already ascertained Gary had not only been alone with Charlotte shortly before her demise, but also already present when Ashwini rushed to help, it suddenly seemed as if I may have missed something terribly important during my little chat with Gary, and I determined at once to find out what it might be.

Chapter Nine

Finbury kept Harry in the meeting room for a while longer, despite Harry's suggestion that Finbury divert his interrogation towards Gary instead.

"I *loved* her," Harry said, every now and then, his voice rising in despair as Finbury did his best to bully a confession from his current witness. "Why would I want to kill her?"

I must admit I felt quite the level of sympathy for the young man, as he became increasingly distraught, and I did not share Finbury's certainty about the matter, even though one might agree there was a certain level of motive. As any reader of Shakespeare and the classics will know – whether they are a retired English teacher or merely a student of such – spurned love can lead one to act in the most extraordinary manner. Moreover, if those clever murder mysteries on the television are anything to go by, a failed love affair is a thoroughly appropriate motive for any manner of crimes. However, I was in some doubt that one so emotional as young Harry would have the wherewithal to carry out a murder in such a quiet and public location as the non-fiction section of a small town's library, although one never knows what one may be capable of when pushed. Or, I thought to myself with a small inward smile at the little pun, when one does the pushing.

Nevertheless, given that I harboured evidence to point far more convincingly in an altogether different direction, I remained open-minded about the whole affair. I have to admit I couldn't find any logical or obvious reasons for Harry's accusation that Gary might be to blame, but nevertheless, as his words tumbled in my mind, I had one of those funny little niggles one gets when one suspects that someone has said something that might help make some sense of it but can't quite put one's finger on the information.

Therefore, as I am sure you will agree, it was imperative to discern what exactly Harry had meant when he'd told Finbury that Gary disliked Charlotte. I racked my brain about it for a while, but I simply could not think of any reason, as I have always found Gary to be perfectly pleasant and hard-working.

I tentatively added him to the growing list of suspects I was collecting in my mind, although however much I wished it to not be the case, I remained quite certain it must be one of the other three: Harry, Isobel, or Carrie, as two out of the three appeared to have a clear and indisputable motive for such, and the other, unfortunately, had been caught in the act, as they say. Not of murder, of course, but certainly of an untruth as to her whereabouts at the time of the crime, and that, I am sure you agree, was suspicious enough in itself. While I am not accustomed to self-pity, I longed to be able to jot my thoughts into a notebook, or at least to drag Phyllis off to a quiet corner where I might get her to be my secretary, even though we had both managed to escape from that particular occupation by persuading our parents to allow us to enter the teaching profession instead. My mother had very much wanted me to make use of my typewriting skills and become a secretary, as many young girls did back then, although she did concede that I had done terribly well, all things considered, when I was allocated Head of Fifth Form at St Cuthbert's, and that perhaps it had been for the best.

I have digressed, but the point of the matter is that Phyllis is remarkably good at taking notes. She has become quite accustomed to writing things down for me to remember on the occasions when I am unable to access the clever little voice-recording contraption on my mobile telephone, and this, you will understand, was one such occasion. Not because I was at all worried that someone may have pilfered it from my handbag, as I mentioned, but because I had no desire to be overheard. I could whisper my thoughts to Phyllis, who has perfectly good hearing despite what she has to say about it from time to time, and she would be able to record the notes with far greater accuracy than were I to whisper into my recording device. I have learned from experience that the device does not function with any degree of clarity if one speaks to it in a whisper.

Indeed, Dennis has not allowed me to forget the unfortunate occasion upon which I attempted to make notes on one particularly gripping book-club choice, despite it being quite some years ago. Even though Dennis is a terribly deep sleeper, and never seems to be disturbed by his snoring – which is quite remarkable as even Donald next door has grumbled about it from time to time – I will listen to my audio device through a set of headphones, if I am in bed, so as not to disturb him. Of course, if I reach a particularly interesting or relevant plot point, I might need to make a note about it, and on one such night, I had whispered my thoughts as softly as is possible into the recorder so as not to disturb him. The next day, an eerie ghostlike hissing had drifted about the lounge, quite indecipherable as a human voice, giving both Dennis and I an awful fright. The whispers permeated into the living room for quite some time, until I got up from the sofa to see if the noise might be coming from the kitchen and Dennis spotted the telephone under the cushion. We immediately deduced that I must have inadvertently and unknowingly sat upon the recording device, triggering it to play the ghostly sounds, which transpired to be none other than my softly-whispered and entirely indecipherable book-club notes.

Thus, I'm sure you agree it is imminently more sensible to have a little word with Phyllis and ask her to be note-keeper whenever the need arises. I hadn't forgotten that we were on pretence of visiting the lavatories, as we had said to Gary, and then hoping to get ourselves a nice cup of tea, so I took advantage of that little ruse to drag Phyl off for a bit of a *rendez-vous.*

"Shall we proceed to the Ladies?" I reminded Phyllis in a whisper deliberately loud enough to be overheard by anyone who happened to be paying attention to the two perfectly innocent older ladies as they wandered through the library. "I am getting quite desperate. And then perhaps you'd make us that tea."

"No chance." Phyl gave quite the dramatic tremor, sending vibrations along my arm. "I'm not going in there while Doofus is there. Perhaps Carrie would pop in and get the kettle out and bring it to the counter? Or Josephine. Sure, wouldn't that be better? She can say Carrie is feeling the shock."

"Phyllis!" Josephine has a deep, throaty kind of laugh, and it gave me quite the start, and caused me to give poor Amity's harness a terrible jerk. It was terribly ironic that Josephine might give me a real shock at just the moment Phyllis had suggested using Carrie's state of shock to gain access to the tea-making facilities, which just goes to show one shouldn't exploit another's misfortune for one's own reward, don't you agree?

Nevertheless, Josephine said all right then, and told us to get off to the loos before I had an unfortunate, which is what Josephine calls it when one of her charges in the primary school has any kind of accident, and off she went to face Finbury and pilfer the kettle out from under his nose.

I don't suppose you'll be at all surprised to hear that I didn't have any need to use the facilities at all, although once we'd got ourselves in through the door, dear Amity tried her best to guide me onwards into the cubicle. When I stopped her, she became quite bemused about the whole thing.

To add to Amity's confusion, Phyllis said she may as well go while we were here, so in she went, with Amity and I waiting in front of the basins. Phyl and I are quite used to conversing with one another through a lavatory door, which is quite a different kind of a thing from one holding a telephone conversation whilst using the lavatory. After two dear friends have shared a room for three years during teacher training college several decades ago, and remained inseparable ever since, they have very few inhibitions around each other. Therefore, as time was of the essence, we conferred in quiet voices with Phyllis attending to her business behind the closed cubicle door, and Amity and I hovering by the sinks in the hand-washing area.

"Salamander Smith," she hissed in the voice she reserves for when she is getting frustrated about something. "Before we even *think* about the information Gary gave us about Harry and Isobel, or what Harry just told Doofus about Gary, will you kindly tell me what *you* meant about her earlier?"

"Her?"

"Sally!" she hissed at me over the faint crumple of a sheet or two of lavatory paper being torn from the roll. "Don't be so infuriating. You know perfectly well who I mean. Isobel, you daft old woman."

"Ah," I said, "I supposed that might be what was on your mind and I am awfully surprised you haven't worked it out. You aren't being terribly sharp today, Phyl."

Her retort was quite unsavoury, so I won't repeat it, but suffice to say she tried to get awfully cross with me but it was somewhat spoiled by the rustle of her getting her trousers up and fastened, the flushing of the lavatory, and the screech of the bolt. I told her if she just finished what she was doing and got herself out, it would be much easier to tell her.

Amity gave a little whine to let Phyl know she agreed, and another to let me know she really didn't understand why I had asked her to bring us in here if I wasn't going to enter the cubicles or utilise the basins, so to appease the poor bewildered creature, I turned on one of the taps and gave my hands a little rinse. That done, I patted around until I found the button for the drier, which appeased Amity quite well, but not Phyllis.

"Sally Smith! You are doing this on purpose."

I said I really didn't know what she meant, and she turned on the tap to wash her hands and I would not be at all surprised if she was making just as much noise as is possible while she did so. The dryer stopped before she got to it, and she said she was blowed if she was going to start it again and she must have given her hands a vigorous shake instead, as a sprinkle of drops hit me full in the face.

"Well," I said, "if you just have a little think and use those little grey cells of yours, you will realise exactly what tipped me off about it all. Think about what Isobel said, right back when Ashwini was first called away."

"Oh for goodness' sake, Sally. *What*?" She flicked another spray of water at my face in a terribly childish manner and there was that swishing sound one makes if one wipes one's hands on one's trousers, and then she said, "I really haven't the foggiest, Sal. You will just have to enlighten me."

"*She*. She said 'she'. Everyone else said *someone* had been taken ill, but Isobel knew it was a 'she' before any of the rest of us knew. It wasn't until a little bit later on when Kimberley went out and came back in again that any of knew it was Charlotte."

Phyllis gave a little gasp and said, "Goodness, Sal," a few times until I told her there was more. At that, she immediately stopped gasping like a carp, and shut up.

"When she got up and said she was popping to the lavatory, you will probably recall that even Kimberly noticed *that* was an untruth."

"Yes," Phyl agreed. "Kimberly said she thought Isobel had nipped out for a cigarette and Isobel admitted to it there and then and said she'd been caught in the act."

"And I believe it must have been Isobel to whom Gary referred? I can't imagine it could have been Josephine, although she was quite the stunner in her younger days, and presuming Mary has managed to describe herself to me with any degree of accuracy, she is terribly pale-skinned. In point of fact, she was complaining about her sunburn when she arrived this morning –"

"Red and white all over, sure she was –"

"– and I don't imagine Kimberly has managed to change colour since I was able to see her, and I may be blind, but I am not deluded and I don't expect for a moment that Gary would have described any of the others of us as pretty young girls, do you?" Of course, I didn't wait for Phyllis to answer that, as it was perfectly obvious and I expect even Doofus could manage to work out who amongst us in the library that day might fit the description of pretty, young, and darker-skinned. "So I think we can agree that it can only have been Isobel whom Gary saw heading into the non-fiction shelves after Charlotte and Harry?"

"Yes, I thought so, too, and isn't that very suspicious, Sal? What on earth was she doing all the way over there and not at all near to the loos?"

"If Gary is telling the truth, I'm afraid it puts her very much in the frame, don't you agree? I can't see any reason to doubt him at this conjecture. There is simply no disputing that Isobel was *not* telling the truth about why she left the room, and she knew before anyone told us that the person in trouble was a 'she', which is altogether suspicious, don't you agree?"

Phyl said yes, she certainly saw my point, and it did make the girl look bad, for sure, but she was such a delicate little thing and so young, and surely I didn't think she could possibly have done Charlotte any harm, did I?

I said I didn't know about her being delicate, but as it seems unlikely that whoever killed poor Charlotte used a heavy object or tackled her to the ground, it might be perfectly feasible if one was taken by surprise and killed in some other way. "And," I added with sudden realisation, "she'd only been back in the room with us a few minutes when all the hoohah started up, which is terribly suspicious, now I think about it."

Phyllis made one of those non-committal disapproving kind of noises that shows she doesn't agree with something but concedes there is some merit in what I have said, nonetheless. After a moment, she gave a little huff and then said, "All right, Sally, supposing for a minute you're right, why on earth would she want to hurt Charlotte? She's a wee dote and does enjoy coming along to the club."

I said I wasn't at all sure I'd call her a wee dote, and I certainly didn't know that reading books about murder mysteries was any kind of endorsement and perhaps it was reading all these murders that had put her in the mind of it and Phyl said not to be silly, then went quiet for a second or two before adding, "I suppose you could be onto something, so the thing we had better establish is *why*?"

"And how. There is also one more thing. Another slip of the tongue, perhaps. I don't suppose for a moment that you have any recollection of what Isobel was worried about after Kimberly informed us it was indeed Charlotte?"

Phyllis didn't say anything, so I guessed at once that she had not paid the slightest attention to that little snippet of information either.

"When everyone was offering their suggestions as to *what* might have happened to cause poor Charlotte's demise, Isobel was concerned as to whether anyone *knew* what had happened."

"We all wondered that," Phyl said, so I could tell she wasn't following the trail of clues at all.

"Phyllis! While the rest of us wondered *what*, Isobel wondered *who might know*. She sounded *worried*. She didn't join the speculation as to the method, only the witnesses thereto. Whether someone might have been found out." I gave Phyllis a poke with my fingers and said, "Amity, take us back to the meeting room. I think it is time we asked Isobel a few questions and had that cup of tea, if Josephine has managed to get round that imbecilic Doofus, don't you think?"

Chapter Ten

Once Phyllis and I had stepped over the threshold between the Ladies and the library, we stopped to get our bearings, in so much as we had agreed it would be a sensible idea to assess who was where and what was being said by whom, before going directly back to the meeting room to confront Isobel. We stood, just outside the lavatory door, frozen and silent, as I tuned into each section of sound around the library. Beyond our meeting room, from which some low chatter emanated, you will not be at all surprised to hear that the over-riding noise came from the loud-mouthed flibbert in the further meeting room.

Whilst Phyllis and I had detoured into the lavatories, it seemed that Finbury had released Harry from his interrogations and replaced him with Gary. At once, I feared it was too late to get anything much from Isobel, as the next thing we heard was Gary relaying the very information he had shared with Phyllis and me.

"I came out after sorting me papers. That young 'un 'ad the librarian up agains' the shelves. That young 'un's been a nuisance to 'er for weeks. 'arassment, you'd call it, most like. In't firs' time she'd asked 'im t' leave 'er be. The other young girl came over – 'ad eyes on 'im about as long as 'ee's been bothering the librarian, if you ask me. She's as bad as 'ee is, only 'ee 'an't noticed, so it ain't 'arassment, then, is it? Why she came over, I coul'nt tell you. Lef' 'em to it. Not my problem wha' she got 'erself int'. Got enough on me plate. Wen' back t' me computer an' got on with it."

From our left, someone said something that sounded very much like, "oomph," which I imagined came from one of the two girls, Mary or Isobel, as I didn't think anyone other than Joan had remained in the Book club meeting room at that point in time and I simply couldn't imagine Joan would make such a noise as that. No one said anything else, and I wondered if the sound had been an involuntary expression of surprise, or perhaps a reaction of fear or guilt. Still, neither girl spoke, nor Joan, and I supposed they, like Phyl and I, might be silently awaiting Finbury's response to Gary's declaration.

However, in his typically inept way, Finbury did not pursue the logical or sensible line of inquiry, and appeared to brush aside Gary's observations as if they were of no consequence to the matter at all.

"I have authority that you have motive to have attacked the unfortunate victim, so I would thank you not to cast aspersions at others," he said in his most bombastic tones. I had little doubt that he had no understanding of half the words he uttered, and this feeble attempt at a coherent sentence was a half-remembered phrase he had learned from one of his Police Training manuals.

"You wha'?" Gary, too, seemed to find difficulty in following Finbury's convoluted instructions.

"Did you or did you not attack Charlotte Lewisham and leave her dead?" Finbury said, his voice as high and shrill as when he spilled a can of coca cola across the fifth-form classroom and blamed his classmates.

"Course I blooming din't. Why would I do tha'?" Gary, by contrast, replied in his perfectly usual tone without raising his voice at all, as if he were slightly dumbfounded by the spectacle of Doofus Finbury attempting to solve a crime. Nonetheless, to my attuned ear, I could make out the very faintest of wobbles and I was quite certain it may be taking Gary a great deal of effort to maintain his composure.

"You tell me. Your friend over there is most insistent that you had beef with the woman."

"Blinking 'eck, Dougal, you learn tha' in college? Beef?" Gary gave a low, dry laugh. "Okay, what've you got on me, 'cause from where I'm sitting, tha' 'arry fella's got far more ... beef ... than me! Or don't your lot mind about 'arassing young girls nowadays? Though' that'd be your big thing, these days."

Doofus retorted that the police had far more interest in murder than in harassment, and Gary laughed again and said wasn't it highly likely that one might lead to the other, and I was in perfect agreement about that as one only has to listen to the news to hear about that kind of thing. Nonetheless, it appeared to be too much for Doofus to process as he had a little harrumph and said, "Perhaps you could leave the police work to the professionals."

Phyllis gave me a sharp nudge and whispered, "Ah now, he's going to call the professionals, Sal."

"Shh!" I dug her in the side, trying to listen, although it hardly seemed likely that Finbury was going to say anything of any use to the matter. However, in a stroke of luck somewhere along the lines of his buffoonery, he had inadvertently reminded me of something pertinent, so I made up my mind at once to deviate back to the library desk before approaching Isobel. "Phyllis, we must speak to Barbara before we go to Isobel."

Of course, she was a little confused by my abrupt change of heart, but we are quite in tune with one another so I'm sure she would have guessed that I'd had a thought about something. Sure enough, she after one of her little huffs, she said, "All right then. I suppose you have one of your ideas." With that, she turned me sharply to the right and away from the meeting room. "We are going straight past **A-E**, directly towards the children's section," she explained, in the helpful way in which she usually guides me from place to place. "We are just about at the staff-only door, and then we will take a sharp left towards the desk. Here we are. About a dozen steps forward should do it. Barbara and Josephine and Ashwini are all there with Carrie." She gave my arm a squeeze and for a moment I almost forgot we were on the hunt for a murderer and were simply going about one of our usual morning excursions about the library.

"It would be quite useful if we could lure Barbara away from the others," I whispered, "but I suppose that might be complicated, so we will have to make do."

"Three or four more steps. Hello again ladies. Sal has a question for you, Barbara." There was a little pause and then she added, "Don't ask me," and her arm rose and fell so I supposed she was shrugging her shoulders and that perhaps

Barbara had given her some kind of questioning look about what it might be that I had on my mind.

"Where are you, Barbara? Perhaps you could give me a little clue, so I don't mistake a pot plant or direct my question to a bookshelf."

"Behind you, Sal," she said, but her voice came quite distinctly from a little to my left, so I knew she was having another of her little jokes.

Doofus's voice reverberated from the meeting room and it seemed as if he might be finishing up with Gary and about to call upon his next victim, so I hastily suggested to Barbara that we duck into the children's section so as to avoid being pounced upon, which had quite the advantage of getting her away from Carrie and everyone, too, don't you agree?

Barbara, as I said, is terribly quick-witted, so she didn't dither about it but merely said, "Go on, I'm right behind you."

Phyllis wheeled me around and off we scooted.

Amity's claws clippety-clipped across the laminate and then fell quiet as we stepped onto the carpet of the children's corner. Her tail beat against my leg as she picked up some interesting scent or the other, but I am pleased to report that the overriding aroma in that section on that particular Tuesday turned out to be neither urine nor bleach, but the altogether more pleasant whiff of sun lotion and chocolate.

"Put me on a seat that is not covered with chocolate smears, if you would," I said to Phyllis, and she lowered me obligingly onto a terribly low chair with a seat hardly large enough to accommodate my bottom, but needs must. Besides, I imagined the alternative may have been one of those beanbag aberrations, from which one simply cannot remove one's self when one has reached the age of seventy-four, so I'm sure you will agree that the child-sized chair was the lesser of the evils.

"Are you sitting too?"

After a little scuffle and a small groan, both Barbara and Phyl agreed they were.

I instructed Amity to sit, and rubbed her ears apologetically. The poor love must have been finding all this rushing about awfully difficult and entirely unexpected, and I made a mental note to get Dennis to take her for a proper walk just as soon as we got home to make up for it all. She really is terribly patient and obliging, but one must suppose that is part of the training, and she is quite used to it by now.

"What I am curious about, Barbara," I said in a low voice, "is exactly what you meant earlier when you said Charlotte was a trouble maker."

"Did I?"

"You did. While we were around the book club table. As it was only about half an hour or so ago, you should be able to remember it quite easily."

Although she rewarded me with one of those little snorts that is not quite a laugh, she didn't say anything straight away, so I expect she was thinking. After a moment or two, she said, "Yes, I did, didn't I." She gave a quiet little sigh. "Shouldn't speak ill of the dead, Sally ..."

"Barbara, you have never minded at all about what you say about anyone," I said.

"Sure, you haven't," Phyllis said. "No point starting now."

Barbara gave a little sniff that I supposed might have been another of those stifled laughs, and for a moment we were just three friends putting our heads together to solve the kind of mystery we discuss in book club, and not a very real and cold-blooded murder of a person we had only spoken with that very morning.

Well, I can tell you that Barbara had quite a lot to say about Charlotte once she got going. Some of it wasn't awfully surprising. Although I have always found the young librarian to be pleasant enough, I'd also harboured the distinct impression that she was the kind of person who would shirk her responsibilities when she had the chance. Shortly, the question was raised once again as to how it had come about that she had received the promotion instead of poor Carrie. Of course, I said it in that musing, rhetorical kind of way, so I was awfully surprised that Barbara had an answer for it immediately.

"Her father is someone in the council. It's all about who you know, Sally, who you know."

I imagined she might be doing that funny little gesture when a person taps her finger against her nose, although I confess, I have never entirely understood the reason for it. Barbara's revelation gave me quite the jolt, and I must say I suddenly felt as if I had been somewhat blind to the full extent of just how hard-done-by poor Carrie must have felt about that, and I don't mean blind in the sense of my day-to-day visual impairment, but in the sense of being an insensitive old woman who had taken Carrie's word for it when she had said she'd got over the disappointment. I'd presumed she really didn't mind about it all that much. She was only a few years from retiring and had told me many times that she was quite looking forward to it, and may even go earlier than she had planned, if her pension would stretch. I supposed I had missed some terribly important, if subtle, little clues of the sort one picks up in facial expressions and body language, when one is observant and has the full use of one's eyesight, and I must say I felt terribly sorry about it. "Goodness," I said. "Poor Carrie."

I had come to Barbara with the intention of asking her about Gary's feelings towards Charlotte, but this latest news added a significant weight to the argument that *Carrie* may in fact have held quite the grudge about her younger and less experienced newly-appointed superior, and thus had a terribly good motive for disposing of her colleague. I didn't want to believe it possible, but one must put one's feelings aside if provided with sufficient evidence. I was rendered quite speechless for a moment as I considered how disappointed Carrie must have felt, and how well she had concealed the fact from me. For a minute or two, I was so boggled by the possibility of Carrie being a killer that I quite forgot about what it might be that Charlotte had done to cause *Gary* any kind of upset.

Finbury's high-and-mighty demands interrupted my train of thought and I guessed at once that he had stepped out of the meeting room, as the increased volume of his voice bounced around the library like an out-of-sequence drumming band. "You may return to whatever it was you were doing, but you may not leave the vicinity. I will call the next person when I am ready."

I hoped Phyllis and Barbara and I might be hidden from his immediate view by some bookcase or the other, as I had no desire to be subjected to an interrogation by Finbury. Phyl and Barbara must have been of the same mind, and with some kind of intuitive silent agreement, neither Barbara, nor Phyl, nor I spoke until the moment had passed and the squeaking retreat of shoes on laminate told us he had taken himself back off into the righthand meeting room to do whatever it was before he called the next of us.

We released our breaths as one, in a funny little collective sigh, and Phyl and Barbara both said, "Phew," in perfect synchronisation, and after we had a bit of a quiet giggle about that, I remembered to ask Barbara if she might have any notions as to why Gary might have reason to dislike Charlotte, as Harry had loudly proclaimed, and another figurative bombshell was immediately dropped.

"She encouraged his wife to leave." Barbara was so matter of fact about it she may as well have been telling us she'd had toast and marmalade for her breakfast, and I had to ask her to repeat herself so I could be sure I had heard her correctly.

"She encouraged his wife to leave him. To up-and-off, if you like. They were having problems, and Jane got chatting to Charlotte about it, and Charlotte said she should gather up her belongings and the children and find herself a nice council house. Charlotte gave her some information and leaflets and a phone number, and a fortnight later, Jane had packed herself up, and the children, and left him. Didn't you know?"

Chapter Eleven

It is not often that I am lost for words, as Phyllis will tell you, but I was momentarily entirely speechless. I imagine I may have gaped like a guppy for a good few seconds before I closed my mouth. Barbara's news had provided a perfectly valid reason for a man to take a dislike to someone, even if that man were as mild-mannered and easy-going as Gary appeared to be, wouldn't you agree? Nonetheless, I couldn't equate the hard-working, kindly man I had encountered a handful of times over the past few years with a cold-blooded killer, any more than I could imagine Carrie doing the deed.

Meanwhile, Harry, by all accounts including Charlotte's own, had certainly demonstrated an unhealthy and unreciprocated infatuation with poor Charlotte, and had behaved in an entirely inappropriate and unpleasant manner towards the poor deceased librarian. However, he had been terribly distraught by her demise and in a great deal of shock over it, and I believe it was quite genuine and not at all artificial. Of course, he might be the kind of person who is quite the accomplished actor, and whilst one must agree that he appeared to be under the impression that the pair were passionately in love, it seems indisputable that Charlotte did not feel at the same way towards him. Nonetheless, given his level of infatuation with the poor girl, it seemed most unlikely that he would want her dead. He had protested his innocence with a great deal of passion, which I had found entirely believable. I am the kind of person who is usually a good judge of a person's character and I had to admit I agreed with Harry's logic on the matter. Whilst he did, perhaps, have *reason* to dislike the girl, he did not, apparently, have done so. I had whole-heartedly believed he was indeed, very much in love with Charlotte; an observation supported by all witnesses to his behaviour over the preceding weeks and months.

All in all, it was impossible to know what to deduce from any of it, and once again, my suspicions returned to Isobel, despite Phyllis's ideas about that. The girl had indisputably acted in a most peculiar manner when she nipped out in the middle of our book club meeting, and more than one witness had placed her in the vicinity of Charlotte's attack. The problem, of course, remained thus: no one had offered any discernible motive for her to have committed the crime. It was most perplexing.

"Hmm," I said quietly, more to myself than to Phyllis or Barbara. "Carrie, Gary, Bel, and Harry. Two people with reasons to dislike Charlotte. Another person who lied about their whereabouts and actions at the time Charlotte died, yet has no apparent motive to have hurt her. One person who was seen cornering the poor girl in the location of her death, yet claims to be in love with her and is clearly terribly distraught about it all. We do seem to be missing something, wouldn't you agree?"

Amity rested her head on my knee and I rubbed her head gently, taking comfort in the silky fur and solid warmth as she blew hot breath across my lap. "What are we not finding, Amity girl? What can you see that I can't? Oh! Maybe that is exactly it." I snapped my head upwards to face towards where I believed Barbara to be seated, and then turned to Phyl, although I could, of course, see neither. "Has anyone thought to search the area in which poor Charlotte was found?"

I had voiced a notion of a book falling from Charlotte's hand, at some point earlier, but I wasn't entirely certain whether anyone had acted on that idea and investigated the area. To my knowledge, no one seemed to have searched for any kind of *weapon*. Charlotte, we had concurred, had not been beaten to death, nor been stabbed or shot. There had, according to both Ashwini and Carrie, been no *blood*. She did not appear to have fallen and hit her head, or to have had any kind of fit, which I presume would have created noise enough that Amity at least, if not any *person* in the building, would have surely been alerted. Ashwini had not mentioned any obvious marks about Charlotte's person as she had attempted to administer first aid, and no one had heard the kind of noise that might indicate a scuffle or fall.

"How," I said aloud, "would one go about killing someone in such silence?"

"And so quickly," Phyllis added.

"And without anyone noticing. Wait there, ladies." Barbara's toddler-sized chair scratched on the rough carpet, and she gave a low groan. A second later, there was that cracking sound one gets from one's knees when rising from an awkward position, and Barbara groaned again. "I don't know how you two will manage to get up," she said, which was a point upon which I had not yet pondered. "Back in a mo."

While she was gone, I allowed myself to tune back in to whatever Finbury might be up to, but blissfully, he was remarkably quiet at that particular moment, and any noise emanating from the right-hand meeting room was too indistinct and distant for me to discern any kind of useful meaning. I deduced that the infuriating imbecile was probably talking to himself.

Isobel and Mary's low chatter drifted from the other meeting room, and I took the time to contemplate what exactly I could say to Isobel to reach any kind of conclusion as to her guilt or innocence. What *had* she been doing in the non-fiction section? Why had she lied about her activities and her whereabouts? And what, exactly, was her relationship with Harry or Charlotte, if any?

"Sal, you are muttering like a deranged harlot."

"Phyllis!"

"Well, you were."

"However would you know what kind of muttering a deranged harlot may utter?"

"Imagination, Sal. Imagination. Now what exactly is it that *you* are imagining to have you so worked up?"

"Phyl, whip out your notebook." I said in a low whisper. "You do have it with you, in that vast bag of yours, don't you? You didn't leave it on the Book Club table?"

She said of course she had it with her, and I had a little chuckle about that as Phyllis is a very practical kind of person, and is never without her handbag. We often have the little joke that she carries the kitchen sink in her handbag, and I wouldn't be at all surprised if she were to pull out a hatstand one of these days, in the manner of Mary Poppins. There was a bit of riffling and Phyllis did some muttering of her own, and a *smmsh* and a shuffle, and then she said she had it, and her pen, and what was it I needed her to jot down?

"Make a list, Phyllis. One. Find evidence. What might be on the floor, or the shelves, or anywhere about the location in which Charlotte collapsed? What would Amity find if she were sniffing about the place and looking under the shelves?"

"I'm not writing all that, Sal. Look. Under. Shelves." As she spoke her pen made faint *rrr rrr* stutters across the pages, and I waited until the noise stopped before I gave the next point.

"Marks on body."

rrr rrr rrr

"Anything paramedics noticed."

rrr rrr rrr

"Isobel. Relationship to Harry. Ditto Charlotte."

The pen stuttered a little more. "Phyllis? Are you using shorthand? Goodness. How terribly clever of you to remember it all these years."

"It's come in most useful since I became your personal note-writer," she retorted, and I agreed at once. "Still, at least I don't have to create Braille for you."

We had a little chuckle about that, as she knows full well that my limited attempts at learning Braille were absolutely hopeless, despite a consternated effort a few years back after Dennis suggested it. "It will open up your world again, Sal," he'd said a little sadly, and I had given it a try, largely to appease him and stop his nagging, but it is terribly complicated when one's fingers want to seek out the Roman alphabet and the complicated little Braille bumps are nothing of the sort. I suppose it's a wonderful system for one who has never become accustomed to reading and learning one's letters, but for me, I'm afraid it was no good at all. Eventually, Dennis agreed that if it were going to make me bad-tempered, perhaps it wasn't a good idea after all. I'd decided I would manage perfectly well with voice notes and recorded material and suchlike after that, and he hadn't mentioned it again.

Phyl's pen stilled. "What next?"

I couldn't think of anything else, and said so, but almost immediately, slapped my hand down in disgust at myself for having forgotten something terribly important. "Phyllis! The window cleaners. Has anyone asked the window cleaners?" I wondered if that was something I must suggest to Finbury, as I was certain he wouldn't think of it himself. The dilemma, of course, would be getting him to take any kind of notice, as he is the kind of person that disregards advice and would trip over his own shoelaces rather than tie them if someone else pointed out to him that they were unfastened.

"Here comes Barbara. And Ashwini. We can start with her."

I supposed Barbara must have had the same ideas about asking Ashwini about any wounds or symptoms upon poor Charlotte's body, but before I could ask about it, Barbara said she'd also sent Kimberly on a bit of a recce of the area, and I had the strangest fluttering in my belly for a second and a wave of something most peculiar. "We are like that little murder-solving group in those Richard Osman stories," I whispered. "It would be terribly exciting, if only Charlotte wasn't dead."

"Then it would hardly be necessary," Phyllis pointed out, and I said I supposed she was right, but it did seem an awful shame, as it would have been a fun exercise for the book group, otherwise.

Finbury seemed to have removed himself from the meeting room once more, as he could be heard quite clearly, booming accusations at Gary, or Harry, or possibly both of them at once, as if they may have conspired and killed the poor girl together. His voice, one would be forgiven for thinking, was loud enough to rattle the window cleaners off their ladders, if indeed they were still upon their ladders by that time. Ashwini, therefore, was able to give us an awfully detailed description of things without danger of being overheard by anyone at all, especially not Police Constable Doofus Finbury.

Of course, she'd told us some of it before, but now I had taken a little more time to gather my own thoughts on the matter, and Phyllis had made a sensible kind of list about it, and Ashwini had partaken of a cup of tea and got herself together after the initial shock, so we were able to go through it quite systematically.

Phyl made a little tapping noise as if she might be jabbing at her page with the point of her pen and said, "Was there any sign of blood?" so I supposed she might be consulting some type of checklist. I imagine she must have had it quite well organised and felt terribly proud of her in that moment. Phyl and I had already considered about the blood, but it was useful to double check the details to be perfectly sure, as we certainly didn't want to miss anything.

"Not that I noticed," Ashwini answered without any hesitation at all.

"She didn't bleed to death, so."

We all agreed quite easily that ruled out any of those stabbings one hears about on the news, or even an accidental gash caused by a fall against a bookshelf or whatnot, and even though we had already presumed that to be the case, it was reassuring to have it confirmed by a doctor's wife.

Phyl went on to the next item on her list. "You said you had checked her airways?"

Ashwini said yes, of course, which was hardly a surprise, as any competent first aider would check for breath in all manner of ways.

"She didn't choke, sure she didn't?" Phyl asked next.

"There would have been some noise. She'd have thrashed about all over the place to get someone's attention." Barbara said. She would know all about that, as she had told us once about some poor friend of her mother's who'd choked on a fishbone in one of those restaurants with a French menu. The poor woman had been terribly embarrassed by it, but we had all agreed it better to be embarrassed than dead, and Barbara had said she supposed so, although she hadn't seemed terribly certain about that.

Across the room, there was the squeak of shoes, then a series of wheezing breaths accompanying the creaks and strains of the corrugated sliding wall being dragged either open or closed. From the unusually restrained volume of Finbury's voice, I deduced he might be talking on the telephone, and wondered if he had, at last, decided to call upon one of his more competent colleagues for assistance. No sooner had I had the thought when Barbara mumbled something about how he was probably calling for a pizza, which gave us a bit of light moment in the midst of our thoughts about how poor Charlotte might have died.

Phyl's pen rumbled across her notebook, and then she asked Ashwini if she'd had to loosen any clothing around Charlotte's neck to make it easier to get at or anything like that, and I must say I felt another swell of pride at how thorough and thoughtful Phyllis had been in her notes. I hadn't thought about the clothing at all, but knew at once where she was going with her line of questioning.

Ashwini said yes, she'd fumbled about with Charlotte's blouse and necklace, and sure enough, the next thing Phyl asked was whether there had been any of that bruising or any funny lines like one might get if one had been strangled by someone.

Either Barbara or Ashwini gave a sharp intake of breath, and Ashwini said goodness no, not even a mark from the necklace, and Phyl said would she have noticed? Ashwini said she thought she would, because Charlotte's blouse was already undone at the top two buttons. She'd pulled the collar away but it hadn't been at all tight now she thought about it. She'd put her fingers on Charlotte's neck to feel for a pulse and there hadn't been anything there at all. Of course, the double meaning of Ashwini's confirmation occurred to me at once, but I presumed her to be answering about the strangulation marks, and not referring to the pulse. Or lack thereof.

Barbara said, "Would you notice if someone had been strangled?" and I said that on those detective shows on the television and in any number of those murder mystery books I've enjoyed on my audio device, there is always a most graphic description of some kind of visible clue when a person has been the victim of strangulation. Ashwini agreed that she thought there would be something, and Phyl said, "Sure, wouldn't there be fingerprint-shaped bruises or a livid pink line where a string or wire or cable yoke from a mobile telephone charging device had been wrapped around the neck, sure there would."

Ashwini must have given quite the shudder at that, as the low child-sized table we were sitting around wobbled as she said, "Goodness Phyllis, you have quite the imagination." Ashwini said nothing for a few moments after that, so I presumed she was thinking it over, and after a minute or two in which none of us spoke at all, she said, "I thought for a minute her face was a bit bruised, but then I realised her make-up was a bit smudged. I think that may have been from Carrie or I as we attended to her, so it was nothing."

It didn't seem as if were making any kind of progress, but before Phyllis could move on to whatever the next item might be, the pattering of footsteps on the laminate neared the children's area. The footsteps softened to become barely audible thuds once whoever it might be stepped onto the carpet. I knew at once it wasn't Finbury, as the footsteps were not in any way similar to the sound one might associate with a stampede of buffalos, nor were there the accompanying squeaks one hears from his shoes or the faint whiff of bacon emanating from his person on that particular day. I also eliminated the possibility of Carrie or Josephine, as Josephine is quite heavy on her feet, and Carrie has a preference for the sensible kind of shoes Phyllis had already confirmed her to be wearing when she peered below the bookcases. One can hear those quite distinctly on the laminate flooring.

Besides, I could quite clearly hear the two of them talking at the desk.

Isobel and Mary were still chattering quietly, too, as their voices carried softly from the meeting room in which we had held our aborted book club.

Therefore, I deduced quite easily that it must be Kimberly approaching. "Is that you Kimberly?" I said in as low a voice as I could manage while still ensuring whoever it was would be certain of whom I was addressing. I very much hoped it was she, and that she might have something helpful to share with us.

"Yes," she whispered. "It's me."

I asked her if she had found anything of interest, and she said there had been a couple of books on the floor, so I had been right about that. She had also found a pen rolled under the shelves, she said, which she'd picked up but didn't see it would be any kind of help so she'd left it on the desk on her way past.

Of course, I wanted to know what the books were, in case they gave any kind of clues as to what Charlotte might have been looking for, as that might help us to narrow it down. I'm sure you will agree that Isobel would be unlikely to be asking about books on steam trains, for example, or that Gary might have been researching the history of ballet, so you can see how it could be useful to know the titles.

To my right, Phyllis moved in her seat and brushed against me, and a moment later there was a soft *thunk* so I guessed she had taken one of the books from Kimberly. To my other side, there came that *flck-flck-flck* of someone fanning through the pages of a book, followed by the louder *thnk* as they closed the book and set it down.

"Garden Design," Phyllis said.

"Encyclopaedia of Victorian Needlework?" Barbara's tone was most incredulous as if she simply couldn't fathom why anyone would have an interest in such a thing, but almost at once Ashwini said, "How lovely," so it just goes to show how different people can be, but it didn't seem to throw much light on who may have killed Charlotte as we all agreed that we couldn't imagine Harry or Isobel or Gary having any interest in such a thing, although I said I supposed Gary might take out a book on garden design. I explained how he'd helped Dennis with our lawnmower and fence and everyone was terribly interested in that and said it looked like perhaps Charlotte was getting something for Gary then. I said one couldn't jump to conclusions, as he really didn't seem like the kind of person who would be interested in Victorian needlework.

Phyl put her lips so close to my ear it felt as if she were giving me a little peck and there was a waft of warm breath and she whispered, soft as anything, "Don't forget Carrie, Sal. She could have done it," and of course at that moment I *had* quite forgotten that Carrie was one of our suspects.

"The books may be one of those red herrings one finds sprinkled throughout our Agatha Christie books," I said to my friends. "We can't place too much hope in them after all. We have been following a notion that Charlotte was helping a reader locate a certain book, but we have forgotten that a librarian must also shelve books that have been recently returned. I suppose Carrie might know if that is the case with these two books, if we ask her."

Everyone fell into one of those thoughtful silences. I supposed we were all wondering whether we had learned anything at all useful, or had, as I very much feared, made absolutely no progress with getting to the bottom of the mystery.

Eventually Ashwini said perhaps we could go back to our meeting room and try to continue with our book group, and Barbara said as no one seemed to have any better ideas, we might as well.

"Sure, we won't get much done about *The ABC Murders*," Phyllis said, "not with all this excitement going on and Doofus making so much noise."

This reminded me at once that we hadn't at all finished with our own list. Besides, something else had occurred to me and whilst I was quite sure it was nothing of any importance, it is sensible to eliminate every possibility, as Poirot likes to remind us. "We should be sure to cover all the ABCs," I said to Phyl in a low voice, and she gave a short little chuckle, at which I gave her a sharp jab in the side with my fingers.

"Ouch!"

I must say she sounded most indignant and for a moment I felt quite irritated with her as she knew full well that we were to speak with Isobel and I didn't see how we could get anything much out of Isobel if everyone else came along.

Fortunately, Barbara must have got the idea that we might do a little more investigating first, as she said she didn't know about anyone else, but she was going to ask that idiotic policeman if it was okay to nip out and get a breath of fresh air as it was very hot in the library. She could bring Amity out for a wee, she said, if she might need one, as it would give her an excuse he couldn't argue with.

"He'll try anyway," she added in that dry wit of hers, and I said she was quite correct about that, but of course she could bring Amity.

Of course, Amity is trained extremely well and is quite used to waiting and I thought we had only been in the library for about an hour and a half altogether by then, even though one would be easily forgiven for thinking we'd been there for a good deal longer. Nonetheless, it was an awfully good idea of Barbara's, and I hoped she meant she would have a bit of a look around the place and see if she could find the window cleaners and have a chat with them, so I said in my normal voice in case Finbury might hear, "Thank you, I am quite sure Amity would be most grateful for a bit of a stretch," and then I dropped my voice to a whisper and added, "and you can have a word with Jeff if he is still about. See if they noticed anything going on while they were washing the windows, as they would have been perfectly well positioned to see something another person might have missed."

I fumbled about with Amity's harness for a minute, and released her from it. "If you pop back to the meeting room," I said to Barbara, "and have a root around in my handbag, you'll find her lead and one of those little bag whatnots although I can't imagine you will need it as she is quite regular in her motions, and Dennis usually sees to it."

Barbara got herself up off the chair again, with almost as much groaning as the last time, and Ashwini got up too, but with significantly fewer complaints, so she must be far more limber than the rest of us. She is also a decade or so younger, so that must be of some help.

I couldn't be sure whether Kimberly had stayed nearby, as I had been concentrating on other sounds and movement around me and had quite lost track of Kimberly, so I said, "Kimberly, are you still here?" in a quiet voice, and I was pleased when she said, "Yes, Mrs Smith, I'm just over here," in an equally soft whisper.

I asked her to pop over and ask Carrie if there was even the smallest off-chance she might know to whom the pen had belonged, just in case it was anything at all different or one of those fancy personalised ones, although of course it was terribly unlikely, and she said it was just a pen but she'd go and ask, and off she went.

As soon as Kimberley had padded off to the counter, I gave Amity the instruction to go off with Barbara. She gave me a little nuzzle with her nose, so I told Barbara to be firm about it and tell her to come, and off she trotted beside Barbara with her claws tippety-tapping on the floor, and a moment later, Barbara announced quite firmly to Finbury that Mrs Smith's guide dog needed to get out for a minute, so she was just going to take her for a walk around the building and she'd be right back in.

It was of no surprise to any of us that Police Constable Finbury harrumphed and blustered about it, but I supposed even he had the sense to realise it wasn't the kind of thing he could object to and it wasn't as if any of us were under arrest or bound to remain in the library. When he'd had another little *humph* about it all, he said all right then but to remain in the vicinity, in the kind of tone that suggested he would very much like to lock us all in until he had got the bottom of things.

A moment later, Isobel's plummy voice said in a timid kind of way that she needed a smoke, and she'd go too, which was not the outcome I had hoped for and threw a bit of a spanner in my plan. I had lost track of whom exactly it might be that Finbury had in the right-hand meeting room at that exact moment, and with Kimberly and Carrie chatting at the desk I couldn't make out another voice from the meeting room at all. I was just thinking about asking Phyllis about it when Ashwini said, "Is that what you found on the floor, Kim? Excuse me, P.C. Finbury, but you might like to have a look at this. It looks very much as if it might be one of those EpiPen things."

Chapter Twelve

The sliding corrugated wall creaked and scraped for a second or two as if it were being pulled much further open than before, so I deduced Finbury was battling with the contraption and attempting to get himself out of the meeting room again. I am sorry to say that I had the rather unkind thought that in order to accommodate his over-inflated ego, he must open it wider than if he were merely inviting Ashwini into the room to show him whatever it was that she had spotted. I was quite correct in my presumption that he was exiting the room, as a moment later there came the thump-squeak-thump-squeak of his spit-polished policeman shoes on the library floor and a most unsavoury waft of body odour.

"What's that then?"

"I think it's –"

"Hand it over." He didn't say anything for a moment, and then he said, "It's just a pen," and there was the metallic kind of clunk one might expect to hear if someone drops a pen onto a library desktop. "Oi! You! Where are you off to?"

"Me?"

"Yes, you. Where do you think you're going?"

"I ... I was going for a smoke." Isobel's voice was quite feeble and I supposed the buffoon was pointing his finger at her and giving her quite the fright.

"You're not. I want to talk to you. He said you are a person of *significant* interest." He put such great emphasis on the *significant* that I wondered if he didn't know the meaning of it. I suspected it might be another of those phrases he'd learned from the police training textbook.

Poor Isobel stuttered and stammered and didn't seem to know quite what to do, but Josephine is a terribly quick thinker when she needs to be, and she must have been there with them all around the desk, as she said with an air of great authority, "I'll take her back to the other room and she can wait there with us until you are ready for her, Constable Finbury."

If there is one thing Finbury likes, it's thinking people are deferring to him, so of course he said, "See that she waits there," and Josephine's heavy thumping footsteps and Isobel's almost imperceptible steps retreated in the direction of the book club room.

I gave Phyl a quick squeeze with which I hoped to convey, "Ooh, didn't Josephine do jolly well," and Phyllis whispered, "Isobel didn't get out after all, so," which shows just how in tune Phyllis and I can be. However, it also left me in two minds about what to do next. Of course, I still wanted to speak with Isobel regarding whatever it was she had been doing in the cookery section when she'd said she was going to the Ladies. However, I also had the notion it would be of great benefit to our sleuthing to loiter in the vicinity of the desk, in case we might be able to hear what exactly it was that Kimberly had found beneath the shelving.

It had been quite some time since I had seen one of those EpiPen contraptions, although in my teaching days, we teachers were quite familiar with them. Two of the pupils in St Cuthbert's were terribly allergic and we underwent an evening of training about it. I wondered whether perhaps Charlotte had suffered an allergic reaction to something, and in her attempts to activate the medication, she had dropped the pen and succumbed to whatever it was, and her death had not been at all suspicious after all. As soon as I had that thought, I experienced the rather uncomfortable niggle that perhaps I'd got a bee in my bonnet over nothing, while poor Charlotte ... well, perhaps poor Charlotte had simply got a bee.

Regardless, I had no intention of bringing Phyllis or myself to Finbury's attention. Phyllis must have felt the same, as we silently agreed to stay where we were for the time being, until he had retreated to the meeting room or back to the police station or to whomever he may go off and annoy next. Of course, that immediately solved the complicated dilemma as to whether to follow Isobel to the meeting room or remain in earshot of the desk, which saved us from having to worry about that. I had guessed we were, indeed, somewhat screened from his view by a shelf unit or suchlike, as I could just about make out a dark shape looming between the main library space and where we sat on our low chairs in the children's section. We stayed quiet, and it is perfectly accurate to say I was not the only one of the pair of us who strained my ears towards the desk to hear what might come next.

"No, look. See, here. This window ... maybe not an EpiPen, as I think they might say so on the shaft, but something like that. I am sure it is some kind of medical device. Wait a minute

..." From the direction in which Ashwini spoke, there came a rapid *click-click*, and she said, "I will ask Dr Patil." Not a moment later, there was a beep and she said, "That was quick," so I guessed at once she must have sent a photo to the doctor on one of those smartphone contraptions everyone seems to use these days. I supposed the beep signalled that he had immediately responded, as it was a similar sound to that of Phyllis's telephone when she receives a message from Frederick. Of course, Frederick is usually asking something terribly banal such as where she has put the milk or whether she has seen his glasses, and not anything medical or of such significance as to relate to an unexpected death in the library.

"It's an insulin pen," Ashwini said, and Finbury gave a dismissive kind of *hmmph* as if it were of no more importance to him than a piece of fresh fruit. "See. Used by diabetics. You know?"

He humphed again, in an irritated kind of manner and then gave a loud sigh, which I can suppose with a great degree of certainty wafted the stale odour of his bacon brunch into poor Ashwini's face. The repellent stench was quite distinctive, even to me, and as you know, Phyllis and I had remained out of the way, perched upon our child-size chairs in the children's area, so were not at all close to the odious man. I had no doubt at all that Ashwini stood near enough to have received the full force. She had, one must imagine, first handed him the medical pen device, and then shown him the message from her husband, actions of which, I'm sure you'll agree, necessitate close proximity.

"Well," he said, "that settles the matter. I don't know why people can't leave medicine to the professionals. Silly girl." I imagine he spun around on his foot to retreat once more to the right-hand meeting room, as there was the shrill squeal of shoe on floor followed by the squeaking thuds of Finbury's spit-polished shoes. I wouldn't be at all surprised to hear it had left one of those black marks for poor Carrie to clean, as if she hadn't quite enough to be going on with. He stomped off towards the meeting room, but it was perfectly easy to hear him calling into his radio whatnot and informing whoever happened to be on the other end of the device that as an insulin syringe had been retrieved from the scene, the deceased appeared to have given herself an injection and that was that.

A loud crackle emitted from the radio and then a fragmented voice spoke in what sounded like a terribly exasperated manner. "Have we conf –" *crackle* "– in fact –" *crackle* "– etic?"

Well of course, Finbury had to ask for it all to be repeated, but to the rest of us, I imagine it was perfectly clear what had been said, and I was quite certain the rest of us had all been thinking it, even without the voice's crackling instruction. When the voice spoke again, it was a good deal clearer and spoke in a careful and precise manner much as one would use if addressing an idiot. "Have we confirmed whether the patient was, in fact, diabetic?"

"Would anyone know about that?" Finbury said loudly. "You? Caroline. You must know."

Carrie gave a sigh, which is a terribly common response when one is addressed by Police Constable Finbury, I can assure you, and said she didn't think Charlotte was a diabetic. She supposed she could look in the files, she said, as they hardly seemed confidential now Charlotte was dead.

Finbury said, "Well, get to it, woman," which was about as rude as one might expect from him, and I said to Phyllis that I had a good mind to report him to his superiors and she said, yes, we really should.

Carrie said she'd just have to get the files up on the computer, and it would take her a minute. After a bit of a wait, she said, "I have her file here." She said it quite distinctly and much as if she were talking to a very young child, or perhaps an intellectually-challenged Police Constable. "No, she hasn't any medical conditions listed. There is nothing to suggest she was diabetic, or severely allergic to anything. She's never mentioned it. I have never heard her refer to a medical issue or seen her with any kind of medication. Not even paracetamol. I really don't think she could have been diabetic."

Finbury huffed at that and said loudly into the room, "Does anyone know? You. You said you are her boyfriend. Was she one of those diabetic people?"

There was a bit of shuffling, and from away on the computer side of the desk, Harry's voice said, "Not as far as I know."

"And you know everything about 'er," Gary called out across the room. "The way you've been carrying on, you woul'nt miss nowt. You'd know if she ain't diabetic, an' you'd most likely know stabbing 'er with a blast of insulin'd kill 'er, too."

I was quite speechless for a moment, as that seemed to settle it once and for all.

Just as soon as I had regained my senses, I patted around to find Phyllis's face. When my hand found her cheek, I put my lips as close to her ear as I could manage without overbalancing off the little chair. "Phyllis," I whispered, as quietly as a breath of warm air, even though I was quite certain we were alone at our little table, what with Ashwini at the desk arguing with Finbury, and Barbara having gone off outside to find the window cleaners with Amity. "We simply must speak to Isobel. I'm fairly certain we have found our killer. No wonder she wanted to do a runner."

"Sally!" she whispered back. "Why ever would she do a runner? You don't still think it was her, sure you don't, not after what we've found out about Harry? And how would Gary know that a jab of insulin would kill someone? That's suspicious, sure it is. I can't say I'd know such a thing –"

I shook my head in what I hoped would convey a most sorrowful manner. "Phyllis O'Leary, you really do disappoint me sometimes. Tut tut, Phyl."

Of course she hasn't been Phyllis O'Leary for a great deal of time, not since she married her Frederick in nineteen-sixty-whenever-it-was, but it is a little something I have picked up from Frederick, who addresses her by her maiden name when he deems her to be behaving in a particularly obtuse manner. She finds it terribly annoying, so it is quite the tease. It started a good deal of time ago, on one of our summer jaunts or another. The four of us – Phyllis and Frederick and Dennis and I – had set out for a picnic and the men had brought fishing rods and it must have been not long after we were married, as none of the children were born. Dennis and Frederick took it upon themselves to teach us to fish, and I must admit I took to it most easily, as my father had taken me as a child, but Phyllis found it terribly difficult and got in quite the tangle. She'd objected most vehemently to Dennis tormenting her about it, and he'd said, "Phyllis

O'Leary, you are quite ridiculous and I don't think we will ever make a fisher out of you."

They must have been still in that glow of bliss one experiences as a newly-wed, as she had retorted that she wasn't an O'Leary any more, and he'd said straight back without even a pause to think about it that he was taking no responsibility for her being so inept at fishing, and she would be an O'Leary when she got in a muddle and a Browning when she got it right. She'd wanted very much to be cross with him and then had the most enormous fit of giggles instead. We'd all ended up collapsed on the river bank in stitches, and Frederick said that had frightened the fish away and we might as well give up and eat the picnic.

"Oh, for pity's sake, Sal, do tell me," Phyl said and pulled me out of my little reverie about the fishing expedition.

"Haven't you ever noticed it, Phyllis? Isobel is a diabetic and has one of those funny little injector whatnots about her person all the time. She told me about when she was asking how it was I'd come to lose my eyesight, as her great grandmother had become quite blind when she was forty-two, and she wondered if I was diabetic too, as that was what had happened to her gran."

"Sally!"

"Shh! We can't alert Finbury. Take me to Isobel, quick-spot."

She got me up off the tiny chair with only a little effort, and as quietly as two slightly-stiff seventy-something women with a hint of arthritis in their joints can manage after sitting in such an unusual position for so long. I had to have a little shake and stretch to get the feeling back, and I expect she did too, and then she led us off to the meeting room. As a matter of precaution, we went around by way of the doorways to the staff-only section and the lavatories, rather than risk being spotted by Finbury. Even one so figuratively short-sighted as he would have been hard-pushed to have not noticed the two of us, had we gone via the desk and the wide avenue in the centre of the library. Nonetheless, out subterfuge paid off, and you will be pleased to know we were entirely undetected and our covert approach entirely successful.

Once we reached the room, we were greeted with the soft rasp of snoring. I deduced at once that Joan must have decided to take a nap. This is not an unusual occurrence during our book club meetings, and we often have to give her a little nudge when it is her turn to say something. Of course, I couldn't blame her on this occasion, as we had rather abandoned her.

At the opposite end of the table, Mary and Isobel were quietly chattering about something or other, and from the lighter side of the room, beyond the window, the trill of birdsong drifted in on the breeze. One might be forgiven for presuming all was well in the world, and no one had been victim to a murder, but I am sorry to say that I soon put a stop to that idyllic notion.

"Who is here?" I said, aiming my question towards the two young students, even though I was perfectly aware of exactly who was present in the room. "Is it only you two and Joan, whom I suspect may have fallen asleep?"

"Just us, and Josephine," Mary said. "Everyone else is over by the desk. Josephine brought you both a cup of tea, but that was *ages* ago now. It's there on the table in front of your chair, Sally. Left a bit. Forward. There! I expect it's cold."

I followed her directions, found the mug, and promptly set it down again so I could fumble about with my chair and pull it out from under the table to sit upon.

"She brought the kettle through here," Isobel added.

I wasn't at all surprised to hear that news, as even Josephine would not relish the idea of speaking to Doofus Finbury any more than she needed in one morning, and as I have mentioned, she is terribly resourceful and the kind of person to think on her feet. I was, however, a little disappointed to realise we had quite forgotten about the tea whilst it was warm, and wondered about asking her to pop the kettle on for a refill.

"Jolly good idea, Jo," Phyllis said, and put me onto my chair and guided my hands back onto the mug of rapidly-cooling tea. "Might you pop the kettle on again and give us a little top-up of hot?"

The two girls assured me that they, unlike Phyl and I, had managed to enjoy both a drink and a biscuit, and Joan had already finished a cup of tea before she gave up and put her head down on her arms and dozed off. Josephine said she'd already had a cup, too, and she wasn't going to be up and down making endless cups of tea all morning while the rest of us got to do the fun mystery-solving part.

I said it wasn't much fun for poor Charlotte, and she said, no, she supposed not. Before anyone could think about that for too long, I continued at great haste, mindful that Finbury could come along and drag Isobel away from us at any second.

"Well," I said. "I am glad you are here. It means you are perfectly placed to answer a few questions before that policeman gets to you. I would be terribly grateful if you would help me understand something."

"Sure," Mary said. "What's up?"

I was not a teacher for the best part of forty years for nothing, and I had already decided that I must employ my strictest no-nonsense tones to speak with Isobel. From the direction of her voice, I deduced her to be seated in the same position as during the book club meeting, and therefore, I turned my face a little to the right of the direction from which Mary had spoken.

"Isobel, I am afraid that policeman is going to ask you some very unpleasant questions in a very unpleasant manner, as it seems perfectly apparent that you have not been entirely forthcoming. It has come to our attention that you did, in fact, speak with Charlotte in the vicinity in which she was found, and I think it might be better if you tell us exactly what you were up to, before Finbury drags you into the other room. He can be terribly impulsive and not at all inclined to hear every possibility before leaping to a conclusion. At this very moment, I have little doubt that somebody will be bringing your name into it all, and I am afraid we may not have a great deal of time."

For a moment the only sounds within the room were a sharp intake of breath from one of the two girls, although I couldn't be entirely sure which; the huffing of Joan's breathing, and the light summer breeze shaking what I supposed might be some of those slatted blinds one sometimes finds in a commercial building. Josephine started to speak, but I held up my hand to ask her to wait.

"Josephine," I said, "I am sure you are about to protest, but I'm very much afraid there is more."

Josephine fell silent at once.

"Given the undisputable evidence that has just been discovered beneath the shelving, it looks very much as if Isobel may indeed have taken it upon herself to do poor Charlotte some interminable harm."

There was a shuddering kind of a gasp and a bit of a stuttering sound as if Mary or Isobel might be about to say something or protest, but I held up my hand again, and they obediently fell quiet.

"Jo, you know as well as I do that Police Constable Finbury is not ... adept, shall we say, in his manner, and just as soon as he finds out that Isobel here carries insulin about her person, he will be popping her into handcuffs before we can say 'sugar'."

"Well," said Josephine, and I guessed at once she didn't know what to say about it. She was quiet for a moment and then said in a feeble kind of voice, "Sugar."

"Isobel, can you tell us why it was that you disliked Charlotte? I wasn't aware that you knew her well." I took a few sips of my cold tea, which was rather unpleasant, so I promptly set it down again and pushed it to one side out of temptation's reach.

Isobel didn't answer the question, and instead, began to cry, at first in quiet sniffles, and then in increasingly loud sobs, punctuated by little bursts in which I guessed she was attempting to protest her innocence, but sounded much as one coming to the end of a bout of hayfever-induced sneezing, with rapid, gasping, intakes of breath and juddering, trembling, sighs. "I–I–I d–d–did–didn't k– k–kill her. I d–didn't."

"If that is indeed the case, I highly suggest you take a deep breath, stop crying, and tell us about it, because very soon,

Dougal Finbury is going to be in here accusing you. Even an incompetent gimlet such as he will piece together you being in the right place at the right time, and having the means to commit the crime, don't you think?"

"Why don't you begin by telling us why you said you were going to the loo, when you didn't go?" Phyllis asked in her kindest and most grandmotherly tones. Phyllis can be awfully gentle when she needs to be, although she usually tries to hide it.

"It was that dishy young Harry, if you ask me." Joan's voice, frail and weak, reverberated into the room like a butterfly's wings beating on a closed window.

I must admit it gave me quite the start, as I hadn't noticed her snoring had stopped, or had any notion that she had woken up.

"Goodness, Joan! I thought you were sound asleep," Phyllis said, so I supposed it had rather taken her by surprise too.

"Just resting my eyes while you were all off beetling about the place and wondering were any of you thinking of returning to our discussion. I had thought about calling that nice young man with the taxi cab to come and collect me and bring me home," she said, her voice quavering like one of those little warbling birds one hears around the garden if next door's cat is safely out of the way. "I can tell you exactly where our Bella went off to. I am quite sure she did intend to go to the lavs, and then she got quite distracted by that luscious young one out there by the computers, as he had not long passed us by to visit the little boys' room." Joan stopped to have a little cough, which one can hardly blame her for as she doesn't often say quite so much in one go, but before anyone else could say anything, off she went again in her tremulous manner. "... but before Isobel was out of her seat, he was back on his way again and if you ask me, he was so darn quick he hardly had time to give his hands a wash so I'd be not so keen to pursue him as all that, young lady, you mark my words." She stopped to get her breath and had another bit of a cough. "Get me a glass of water, won't you lovey."

Of course, I couldn't fathom to whom she addressed the request, but there was the rubbing of a chair across the carpet from the vicinity of Isobel and Mary's corner. I highly doubted it was Isobel who had moved, what with her being under attack as it were, so I supposed it must be Mary who was on the move. Sure enough, a moment later, the scent of orange-blossom drifted behind me, and the door to the lavatories opened with a swish. I couldn't imagine where she might expect to find a glass in there, but I supposed she had an idea about it so I held my silence.

Joan got over her fit of coughing and carried on. "... and off she trotted after him. Preening and puffing like a peacock, you were, patting at your hair and tugging at your blouse, and he went out the door and you went right on out after him, so I suppose that's why you had a cigarette, so you could chat to him, eh?"

Isobel gave an almighty and most inelegant sniff. "He hadn't gone out, in the end, but he'd gone right near the door and I thought he was going to ... I felt all stupid about it, like, didn't I? So, I had to pretend I was going out for something, or he'd have known I was following him, and the window cleaners were leaning up against the wall round the side, having a ciggie, like?"

We all made the kind of encouraging noises that indicate one should continue with one's story.

Isobel took another of those shuddery kinds of intakes of breath and went on. "They gave me that look, and one of them whistled a bit, and I'd normally get angry about it and give them what for, but then I thought I may as well just bum a ciggie off of them, and one of them lit me up and I had a couple of drags, like. Just enough to look like that was why I'd gone out, was all, and then they went back off around the back, and I came back in. That cow Charlotte was over at the back, and Harry got up from by the computer and went after her, and Carrie had her arms full of books and saw me come in, and the phone started up. Carrie looked at me and she looked over to where Charlotte was, and she looked at Harry going after her, and back at me and the phone. Then she answered the phone, said hang on, and asked me would I mind just passing the books over to Charlotte on my way –" Isobel broke off, and had a bit of a sniff and then off she went again. "She knows I like Harry," she said a little sheepishly. "So I took the books off her and took them to over to the corner, only by the time I got to them, Harry had her up against the wall, like."

Someone gave a little gasp and Phyl gripped my knee with such force it was all I could do not to wince.

"– not like he was hurting her, but like she wanted to get past and he wasn't letting her. She clearly isn't into him. If he'd just open his eyes he'd see there's other girls who'd be happy to be with him. She's not good enough for him at all." Isobel's voice became quite hard at that, and for a moment I could quite imagine she might well be able to stab someone with a knitting needle or whatnot, although her venom seemed to be directed more at the object of her affections than at her rival, don't you agree?

"But then I didn't know what to do, because, like, girl code."

I must admit I wasn't entirely sure what she meant by that, but I think I got the gist, and sure enough, when she explained what she did next, it seemed my interpretations were correct, as if Isobel is to be believed, she came to Charlotte's rescue despite her misgivings about the poor girl.

"She clearly wanted out," Isobel said, "even though he weren't hurting her or touching her, or anything like that, so I said, 'Excuse me, Charlotte, but Carrie said give you these', and it is quite true that I don't like her, but only because I fancy the pants off Harry and he's never looked twice coz he's too busy chasing after her and she really isn't interested in him at all anymore and she said ages ago she'd be perfectly happy for me to go after him, if it got him out of her hair. Which was nice of her, I guess." Isobel sounded a bit grudging about it, but it was understandable, in the circumstances.

"She was all right, really, Bel." Mary's soft voice came from somewhere just behind me, so I supposed she'd come back with Joan's water, although Joan had stopped coughing by that point.

"But anyway –" Isobel continued as if Mary hadn't spoken, so I supposed she might not entirely agree on that point. "I held out the books for her to take. She stepped around from Harry, and he shifted a bit to the side and I swear to God he still didn't take his fricking eyes off her and look at me, and I thought I'd give him a little accidental-on-purpose bump to see if that did the trick." She gave a funny little laugh that didn't have any kind of humour in it. "I reached in by him to give the books over, like, and the books on the top of the stack fell off. He launched towards me to try to catch them, but some fell anyway, and then my fricking bag and everything fell too, which wasn't part of the plan." She gave another feeble little laugh and I supposed she might be feeling a bit of a silly about it all. "We all bent down at once to pick them up, and he actually laughed at that and said he'd get it and don't worry, and I felt my whole fricking face go hot so I just grabbed my things as fast as I could and left them to it. Honestly, that's all that happened, it really is." She was quite breathless by the time she had said all that, and I wondered whether I had managed to keep up with all the information she had spieled out upon us, but there was one terribly pertinent piece of information she had omitted to share, and it was that I addressed as a matter of utmost urgency.

"Isobel," I said, in the exact tone of voice I would use when I was trying to get to the bottom of exactly who had drawn a vulgar picture on the black board. "Where is your insulin pen right now?"

"Right here in my bag, of course," she said, without missing a beat.

Chapter Thirteen

Before I could ask Isobel if she were quite certain of that fact, there was a cheery, "Yoohoo!" from the window side of the room, somewhere behind Josephine, I should think, and then Josephine said, "Ouch," followed by a thoroughly unpleasant word.

Immediately thereafter, Barbara's voice said, "Amity has had a lovely little sniff around, and a piddle, and we are just coming back in now. Window cleaners are here, alright. Caught them having a little nap and a fag break, so if there's anything else you want to know, get them now before they bother their pretty little backsides to get back to work, eh lads?"

"Oi. A'right, Ladies?" Jeff's voice was loud and clear, so I supposed he had come at once to the window when Barbara said about it. "Barbara says you's been asking if we're still at it. Takes us a good couple hours to get round. Almost done now."

"Hey love," came another male voice, from the same kind of direction, "cheer up. Want to pop out for another ciggie? You hardly touched yer first one. Give us a smile, eh? It might never 'appen."

I didn't recognise the second voice, although I imagine even Finbury would manage to deduce it to be Jeff's window-cleaner partner, but before any of us had a chance to respond, there was a bit of a thwack, and another "Ouch."

Barbara's sharp voice said something about how it was not the done thing to speak to young girls like that and it wasn't the 1980s anymore. "Apologise to Isobel," she said, "or I'll report you to the policeman who is, at this very moment, sitting inside the library with his handcuffs dangling and looking for someone to use them on."

"Ooh, like that is it now, love?"

"I'm serious, Michael. Sort yourself out."

"All right, Babs, keep yer hair on. Sorry love, didn't mean nothing by it, did I. Just banter, in't it."

During the exchange, I had been gratified to notice that although the window cleaner had been distinctly lacking in that newfangled political correctness that seems to have taken over, he had managed to corroborate at least a part of Isobel's story, in that she had joined them for a cigarette, which she had only half-smoked, as she had also said.

"Jeffrey, Micheal," I called towards the bright, rectangular patch where the window lightened the dark fuzzy greys of the room. The brighter area was broken now by a large shadowy bulk that shifted and swayed, which I deduced to be the two men. "Did you notice anything unusual as you went about cleaning the windows? Which parts of the library can you see into?"

"Eh? What's that Mrs S?"

"Any place there's windows, ain't that right, love?"

I ignored Michael's flippant remark and repeated my question in the direction from which Jeff had spoken. Jeff is quite diligent when he needs to be and appeared to be giving my comments his full attention as far as I could tell from his tone. To the best of my knowledge and memory, and presuming there had been no major changes over the past fifteen years or so, there are wide windows to the front of the library building, which throw a good deal of light into the computer and children's areas. There are similarly large, wide windows at the back, one of which Jeff and Michael appeared to be leaning into and speaking through at that precise point of the proceedings, and another next door in the other meeting room.

"I believe there is also a small, high window in the Ladies' lavatories, as it throws a little rectangle of light into the hand-washing area, but I can't claim to have any idea about the Men's, of course," I said in the general direction of where I imagined Jeff might be peering in through the meeting room window, his elbows resting on the sill, or whatnot, although of course he could have had his hands on his hips or on the handle of his bucket or any manner of poses, but one has to allow some artistic licence when one can't actually *see* a person, don't you agree?

"Blimey, love, first it's harassing a pretty young girl you're accusing me of, and now we're a pair o' peeping flipping toms." It was not Jeff's voice, so I deduced it was Michael who spoke up, and I must say he sounded terribly annoyed. "We ain't peeping toms, if that's what you're getting at."

It took a moment to calm him down after that, although I was quick to say I had implied nothing of the sort. "Someone," I explained, "has died in the library this morning. We are helping the police to see if we could piece together what had happed to her."

Michael quietened down quite considerably at that, and then Jeff said, "So that's why the ambo came, and that pratt Finbury, eh?" and Michael said, "Who'd ha' thought it?" which summed up the morning quite well if you think about it.

There was another pause, in which I quite imagined them to be standing framed by the window, scratching their heads bemusedly, and looking for all the world like those Chuckle Brothers my children enjoyed on the after-school television programmes when they were small. Of course, this was all in my imagination, and they may not have been scratching their heads or indeed looking at all bemused by anything, but it was an amusing interlude in a serious situation. Then one of them said, "Who was it?"

"Do you mean who died, or who did it?" Barbara's voice came in through the window, and I quickly adjusted my mental image by nudging the two men to the right and popping her there beside them, on the left of the window from my position on the inside.

"Well, both, I s'pose, eh?" Jeff said.

"Charlotte. You know, the young librarian," Barbara said. "And the whodunnit part's what we want to find out."

"Pat's daughter? From the council?" I supposed it must be Michael who said this, as it didn't sound at all like Jeff's voice.

"Her? That's who you mean, eh? She's never gone and popped it? Blimey."

Barbara said yes, that's who, and the two window cleaners said something that I will interpret as "goodness me." Their exact words were far more uncouth than that, but one must allow the occasional obscenity to slip out in times of shock, one supposes.

"She looked pretty het up when we were just finishin' the other room a'right," Michael said, although he didn't seem to be terribly perturbed by any of it, which I thought was a little odd, but perhaps he was in some kind of shock, or simply the kind of person who remains laid-back about things, no matter how unusual they might be.

"Which room, and what exactly do you mean by 'het up'?" I said, towards the open window.

"One next door."

"He's nodding towards the other meeting room, I think," Phyllis said helpfully. "Do you mean the one that joins to this one?"

"Aye, that's the one."

"Het up how?" Josephine asked, so I supposed she had realised he hadn't answered my question and I was terribly grateful to her for repeating it.

"Were having a right barney. S'prised you coul'nt hear 'em. Looked like she were having a right go at someone. Or someone 'aving a go at her. Hard to say."

"Handbags at dawn, it were," Jeff added.

"Dawn?" I said, although of course I knew it hadn't been any such time.

"Well, no, not really." Jeff said. "We weren't here 'til same time as you, remember. Came in when yous were at the counter. T'other one came out front with me, showed me where to drop the missus's books. Besides, t'were a fair bit after that, to tell truth."

Of course, once he reminded me, I was quite clear about their time of arrival at the library that morning. Nonetheless, I remained entirely *unclear* as to who had been arguing with Charlotte in the meeting room, and when. Moreover, as he had pointed out, I couldn't at all fathom why we hadn't heard them, whoever they were.

"Who was it in the room with Charlotte?" I said.

"Ah now, that's trouble, in't it. Couldn' tell you. Only Charlotte were in view of window, like, and t'other fellow – or lass – were kinda hid by the shelf in corner. She were standing facing t'wards it, and t'other person were in behind it. Face like thunder on 'er, there were. An' then she stormed out, and what with show over, we hoiked up the gear and moved on to side of building, eh Mike?"

"Aye, right enough."

"What time was that?" I said, although I supposed they might not be the kind of people who pay very attention to such matters.

"Good while back, should think."

"Aye, but fair bit after we started. Middlin', like."

"'bout halfway, should reckon. We do front first, then round side – not much to do there – then the room you women was chinwagging in – this one, that'd be, an' on to next one along. So time you seen us, yeah? Add ten minutes or so, should think. Single window round t'other side after back, and up onto roof for skylights. Ain't done them yet. Leave top t'end, we do."

"Aye. Tricky, that," Jeff agreed. "Up ladders an' all."

"When did you take the break?" I asked, wishing I could make a little note about it all, to get it quite straight in my mind, as I must say it seemed terribly complicated.

"Ah, now there's a question, Mrs S. What'd you reckon, Mike?"

"After two back ones," Mike said without hesitation. "We'd just finished up with second one. Were right hot, so it were. I needed a slash – pardon my French ladies – so I nipped inside to use the jacks, and out again for a smoke, 'fore we got back onto it."

Well, that was an interesting little snippet of information as it placed the window cleaner called Michael in the Gentlemen's lavatories at about the same time as Joan had seen Harry going in and out, so I asked her if she'd noticed that too, and she gave a terribly childish giggle about it and said she'd seen him come and go all right, but as he weren't the looker the other young fellow was, Bel hadn't jumped up to go after him, had she?"

"Was anyone else using the Gents when you were there?" Barbara asked, and there was another slap, which I very much hoped was someone slapping their hand against their leg or some such harmless movement and not the sound of one person striking another, but it was followed by a deep, bellowing guffaw and Jeff said, "They's got you to a tee, mate. Leching after young ones. Peeping tom, and now one of them fellas who looks at other blokes in the jacks! Wait till your missus hears what you get up to on the job."

Any attempt from Michael to respond to the accusation was lost in another bellow of laughter, but eventually they quietened down enough to allow Michael to answer Barbara's question without too many interruptions from his colleague.

"Young fella come in as I went out. Coul'nt tell you who. Take no notice of Jeff. Don't know his you-know from his whatsit, he don't. I ain't like that. Din't talk to him, just stopped door swinging in his face and that were it. Foun' Jeff round side, smoke lit up an' all. Had one too. Seemed fair enough. Can't let a man smoke on his own; ain't right."

"I guess that's about when I came out, then," Isobel said in a quiet little voice. But it can't've been me arguing with Charlotte, can it, as I saw her in by the non-fiction books, not in the meeting room? She must've been arguing with someone before she was in non-fic, so it can't have been Harry, either, as he was at the computers and only went to her just when I was coming back in, and I stopped off to get those books off Carrie, and went over after that, like?"

"Could've been *after* you saw her. She could've gone into the meeting room, argued with someone, and then went *back* to the non-fic where someone killed her," Barbara said, and she had a point, so we really weren't any further on at all after that.

"Isobel," I said, "Would you say that Charlotte was very distressed? When you rescued her from Harry?"

"She'd been crying a bit," Isobel said, and I must say I was not at all surprised to hear this, as I had remembered the little snippet of information Ashwini had mentioned about Charlotte's smudged make up. Nonetheless, one couldn't help deducing that any number of interactions throughout Charlotte's morning could have driven the poor girl to tears, by all accounts, so it hardly seemed to have any bearing upon who her killer might be.

The window cleaners went off to finish putting away their ladders and whatnots and whatever else they had to do to tidy up after themselves, and Barbara said she'd be back in with Amity in a jiffy, and Joan said this was all very dramatic, but that our Hercule Poirot chap would've solved the puzzle by now, and we weren't very good at it were we? She wondered if that bolshy detective fellow would want to speak to her and she didn't feel at all inclined to help him as she'd met his type before, and we all went a bit quiet so we could see who Finbury was going to torment next.

Chapter Fourteen

Finbury took Ashwini into the meeting room for her turn facing his bacon-breathed interrogation, which, as Barbara said sometime later that afternoon could be a good technique for the MI5 chaps, or introduced as one of those torture-type interviews one hears about on the news from time to time.

I couldn't think why Doofus hadn't taken Ashwini in first, now I thought about it, as she seemed to know as much as anyone about the discovery of poor Charlotte's dead body. It was also quite clear that Ashwini was a perfectly innocent bystander and was one of the people in the library about whom we were all in perfect agreement could not possibly have committed the dastardly deed, as it were. Ashwini tends to speak rather softly, unless she is excited about something, so I couldn't pick up anything useful from her side of the conversation, although that may have been because she wasn't saying anything very much, come to think of it.

Once I gave up trying to make out anything Ashwini may or may not be saying, and honed in on Finbury's side of things, I deduced at once he might be talking to someone on the telephone and not to Ashwini at all. After a moment or two of Finbury's usual kind of bluster, during which he placed particular emphasis on such words as "Hypo" and "coma" and "pulse" as if he were reciting from a medical dictionary, I guessed it might be Ashwini's husband, the warm-handed Dr Patil, to whom he was speaking.

There didn't seem to be much to learn from that, so I sat back in my seat and let the events wash over me for a minute, thinking of what the window cleaners had said, and what Isobel had said, and what everyone else had said, and I decided it couldn't be so certain that Isobel was the culprit after all, as it really didn't seem at all plausible that she were the person seen – or not seen, to be accurate about it – arguing with Charlotte in the meeting room and I realised I was still missing some key parts of information.

"Josephine," I said, "would you mind terribly describing the other meeting room to me? You've been in and out all over it making all those lovely cups of tea and I suppose you got the plates for the biscuits from somewhere in there too, now I think about it, so you are perfectly placed to know its layout, wouldn't you say?"

"It's the same as this one," Phyllis said.

"Except the kettle," Mary added.

"And the window," Joan said, and I said yes, we'd discussed it before, and isn't that why we prefer to use the left one, but two people have just referred to something I hadn't realised was in that room. I wondered if it is something I have missed, or perhaps it's been moved quite recently so none of us were aware of the changes.

"If I'm not mistaken," I said, "didn't the window cleaners say that whoever it might have been to whom Charlotte was talking was out of sight behind a shelf, and the last time I was aware of any such thing – well, to be perfectly honest about it, there was no such thing." Everyone gave a little chuckle at that little play on words, but then I continued with my thoughts before we all went off on a tangent about that. "What I mean is," I said, "that I far as I am aware, there is no such shelf protruding into *this* room, and as far as I recall, there is also no such furniture intruding into the other, or I am quite certain one of you would have told me about it, to avoid any danger of bumping into it, don't you agree."

"You're right, Sal," Josephine said. "They've moved the microfiche machine in there, because of a leak by the front window, and some work being done. Carrie got it moved a week or so ago, I should think ... I'd say it was in there the last time I did the teas, and that wasn't last week, because I wasn't here last week, but not the time before that ..."

"It's only the size of the photocopier, though, or thereabouts?" I couldn't fully recollect the size of the contraption as it was an awfully long time since I'd had need to utilise such a thing, and a good fifteen years since I'd *seen* one. "I can't recall it taking up a vast amount of space."

"All the files that go with it are in there too, and they kind of stick out into the room to make a little alcove bit, which I suppose is what Jeff meant when he said about someone being in behind it, as those filing cabinet must be five foot high or more, and there's some stuff piled up on top, too, so you'd be hidden well enough from the window if you were in there using them, for sure."

Well, that gave me something to think about, as I was sure someone else had been talking about the microfiche machine earlier that morning, and I had to rack my brains for a minute or two until it came to me. "The American," I said.

"What about her?" Phyllis said.

"She was using the microfiche contraption. I had presumed her to be located in the computer area near the front window whilst doing so." As soon as I became aware that the contraption was not in the location in which I imagined it to be, it threw an entirely different light upon some of the information April had shared about where she had seen Charlotte and Gary and Harry. "If the microfiche machine had been relocated to the meeting room, then April must have been therein whilst using the contraption, don't you agree?" A response was entirely unnecessary so I did not await such a thing. "Therefore, some of what she'd seen and heard might have a new context if it were in a different place." I needed to take a few minutes to get it all straight in my head, and realised at once that perhaps April might be of some help in determining with whom Charlotte had argued. "Phyllis," I said, turning my head towards my friend, "I think we need to have another little word with April, don't you agree?"

I really was beginning to think we were no closer to solving things than Doofus Finbury, and I couldn't help wondering if perhaps we should simply continue with our book discussion, or call an early finish to the day's meeting. Phyl and I could make the most of the warm day to take a stroll along the high street and around the park, before having a nice lunch in one of the cafes. I said as much to Phyllis and Josephine said perhaps she'd join us. Barbara said she hadn't anything else on that afternoon, so she'd tag along too, and then Finbury's voice cut right across our debate and we changed our minds immediately.

"After carrying out my preliminary investigations, I can assert we are looking at a homicide in the library. It seems most likely that the perpetrator remains present on the premises and I am close to making an arrest. Back up required to contain the suspect."

It didn't take any kind of Poirot or Marple to realise he was, at last, calling his superiors, although, once again, I had quite the suspicion that he was reading from a police handbook as he did so. Nevertheless, the sentiment of his words sent a little shiver down my spine. I deduced at once that Phyllis had the very same reaction to the news, as her cup gave a little rattle on the table top. I must say I was surprised she still held it, as the tea was quite cold by that point, unless she had already drunk it, in which case she also had no need to maintain her grasp of the cup, but Phyllis is one of those people who likes to have something to fiddle about with when she is thinking. I could envisage her quite clearly in my mind, absently turning the mug between her hands while gazing dreamily into the mid-distance. Of course, the Phyllis I imagined in my mind's eye was the Phyllis of fifteen years ago or thereabouts, and I supposed she had changed a little in her appearance. She often likes to tell me her hair has gone far less grey than mine, and she displays fewer wrinkles, but I do not think for a moment that she being entirely truthful in the matter. In fact, Dennis has assured me the opposite is more accurate, although one must assume he may have a certain bias toward me, so one really can't be sure either way. It is fortunate that I am not a vain kind of person, and whilst Harriet does her best to be sure I don't leave the house with egg on my blouse or toothpaste on my collar, I cannot say for certain whether my socks are of a matching colour or not.

While I was wondering about my socks, and just thinking I might ask Phyllis to have a look and let me know about them, Finbury terminated his telephone call.

"I'll see to it at once," he said, at a volume one might hear in the neighbouring village, and most unsuited to a library. He squeaked into the main room once more, and did his unsuccessful best to gain our attention. "Pay attention, everyone," he squealed into the library. "I have an important announcement to make."

Of course, he was quite ineffectual in his efforts at such. I could make out the tap-tapping of a keyboard, the faint hum of at least one of the machines somewhere beyond the desk, and someone other than Finbury speaking into a telephone. The opening of the library door and the familiar clickety-clicking of a dog on laminate floor announced the return of Amity and Barbara, and the low and distant banter of Jeff and Michael drifted through the open windows.

"Ahem," Finbury said in a loud and blustering kind of a way. " I am an officer of –"

"Oh for goodness sake." The voice was Carrie's and it held a most impatient tone. "What is it, Constable?"

"I have been instructed by the superintendent to advise everyone that no one is to leave the premises until a back-up unit arrives, and therefore I must demand you all to remain exactly where you are –"

Phyllis gave me a sharp little poke at that and I knew at once what she was thinking. I could quite imagine us all freezing on the spot like children in a playground game, and it was all I could do not to giggle.

"No further interviews will take place until a second unit arrives. Everyone is to remain calm and you may go about your business of reading or whatever it is you are doing that does not pertain to social media or broadcasting details of the incident."

"What did he say?" Mary asked, and Kimberly said, "No idea, but I think he meant we can't go anywhere and someone more sensible is coming to sort things out."

"A slug would be more sensible," Barbara said, tucking Amity's lead into my hand. "Here you are Sal, one dog safely returned. She's a darling."

Amity settled immediately at my feet, resting her soft head against my ankles in that reassuring manner she has, and I gave her ears a little rub to let her know I was glad of her presence.

Across the library, someone said something I won't repeat, and the American said surely she couldn't be held against her will. Gary said she probably could, but the copper would probably not be much use in stopping her if she left, and April said surely he couldn't think she had anything to do with it. Barbara muttered that he couldn't think at all, but I can't imagine April would have heard that, not from the other side of the room. However, she must have decided not to try to get out in the end, as I could make her out talking to Carrie a little later, so I supposed she was going to grin and bear it like the rest of us. I said to Phyllis that we must go to her at once, as now I realised she had been in the back room to use the microfiche machine and not at the front window as I had presumed, I wanted to ask her about something she had mentioned earlier.

Phyllis said she was altogether worn out from dragging me about the place and she'd go and fetch the American and bring her over to us instead. That way, she said, April could meet the rest of the group while she was at it, which might be nicer for her than sitting over at the computers all bewildered like a fish out of water, which was a kind thought and I agreed at once. Phyl pushed back her chair, patted my shoulder, said, "Back in a jif," and off she went, which gave me time to ask Isobel about another pertinent matter that had been left unfinished.

"Isobel, perhaps you wouldn't mind checking your bag. Of course, if your insulin pen is there as you say it is, it puts quite a different light on the matter, unless you are one of those organised people who carries more than one?"

She said no, she usually just has one with her. She manages the whole thing quite well, she said, and has an app on her phone to help her monitor things. "It's quite a faff at times, but I'm used to it." She gave a heavy sigh and there was a rattle and a clatter of items spilling across the table top, so it seemed as if she had been compliant in searching her bag. I thought that might be either a sign that she was innocent after all, or perhaps a sign of being resigned to her fate, so it hardly seemed conclusive, I'm sure you will agree.

"Oh." There was a good deal of scraping and clattering and the sound of things being moved around across the table and she said, "Oh," again. There came the rubbing about of a heavy kind of fabric, and a bit more of the scraping things on the table, and then she said in a very quiet little voice that sounded quite defeated, "It's not here."

Chapter Fifteen

Of course, everyone reacted in a different way.

Mary uttered a word most inappropriate for the library, although I agreed wholeheartedly with the sentiment if not the language.

Josephine said quite calmly we mustn't jump to any kind of conclusion as Isobel seemed genuinely surprised by the discovery, and Barbara said, "Can one discover a thing that is not there?" with her usual flippancy and quick-wit. Josephine said she had worked in schools quite long enough to know things were never as straightforward as they seemed, to which Joan replied, "Innocent until proved, dearie," in her croaky voice.

Just about then, Phyllis came back with April and introduced her around the table.

After a brief interlude for the pleasantries, I explained to April that I had got a bit confused about something, as I hadn't been at all aware that the microfiche machine had been moved. "When Carrie and Charlotte had been showing her how to use the microfiche contraption," I said, "had you, in fact, been in the meeting room and not in the computer area?"

April said did I mean the little room next door to this one, and I said yes, and she said yes, and I asked her if Gary had been in the room too, and had she happened to notice about the window cleaners?

She said it might have been about the time the window cleaners came along, as she didn't think they'd been there when she first went in, but were there later. The bearded guy had been in there, too, she said, but by the time she came out, he'd gotten back to his computer. The two librarians had left her to it once she'd figured out it was quite easy to use after all. She'd gone back to the computer to check something, and then back to the microfiche, so it was probably then that she'd seen Charlotte talking to the good-looking younger guy. "I walked past the rows of books to get there and back, so I guess I spotted them while I was at it."

I asked if she could recall anyone having any kind of argument with anyone, and she said did I mean the two librarians or the young guy and the deceased librarian.

"Either of them," I said at once.

She didn't say anything for a second or two so I guessed she was getting it straight in her mind before she committed anything aloud. "That young one seemed to be generally bad-tempered with everyone," she said after a moment. "She was awful snippy. I hadn't liked to say so. Everyone else is just awesome. But I guess you have bad apples here too, all right?"

"I guess we do," Barbara said, in the very faintest of American accents, which was typical of Barbara. I very much hoped April didn't think her to be another of the bad apples, as Barbara's heart is in the right place once you get to know her.

Nonetheless, there was something far more pertinent than Barbara's mocking of the visitor, so I nipped it in the bud by asking April if she had meant Charlotte or Harry or someone else entirely when she'd said, 'the young one'. "You used that term earlier when referring to Harry," I reminded her, "and I'd like to be perfectly clear as to whom you now refer."

"Oh," she said, "the librarian. And the dishy young guy. They were at each other like rats in a cage. Lovers' tiff, perhaps."

I asked her if she had any notion as to the time she may have come across the upset.

She had another little think, and no one else said anything either, once one discounts the noise of Finbury huffing about something or other in the next room. It was most unusual for certain amongst us to hold their silence, but I supposed everyone was waiting with bated breath to hear whatever it may be that April was going to say next, in case it was in any way incriminating or exciting.

After a moment, April said she said she really couldn't be sure at all, which I imagine was quite the disappointment to us all after the suspense. "Come to think of it, I must've traipsed back and forth a coupla times, as I'd had to ask if I could print something, and check something else, and suchlike. Can't say I was thinking too much about it, just getting on with it, kinda."

"And Charlotte was still there somewhere?" Barbara piped up again from the far side of the room. "As in, on her feet and not popped her clogs?"

"Popped her clogs?" April's voice held the same confused tone she'd used upon her return to the computer section after her unfortunate experience of being interrogated by Little

Wittering's most incompetent police constable, so I guessed at once that she had never heard that particular idiom before.

"Dead." Phyllis said, which was rather blunt if you ask me, but I suppose it was better to be entirely clear about the matter. "You didn't see her lying on the floor or hear any kind of scuffle?"

"Can't say I'd noticed anything like that ... I'd sure've noticed ... you just would, wouldn't you?"

Josephine asked April if she was usually an observant kind of person, and she had a bit of a think about that while everyone waited in what I presumed to be one of those breath-bated silences, although a bird was chirruping somewhere beyond the window. Finbury, you won't be surprised to hear, was still bleating away in the other room, but I think we'd all had quite enough of him by that point and were all doing our best to blank him out.

"Gee, I guess I must be. I spotted that medipen and picked it up off of the floor, didn't I?"

My ears pricked up immediately. That was quite the surprising piece of information. It had only been a few minutes beforehand that Kimberly had told us *she* had found the medical device, so I didn't know what to make of it at all.

April carried right on talking as if she hadn't said anything at all out of the ordinary, so that gave me a little bit of time to process it.

Phyl, however, gave me my foot a poke with her toes, so I supposed she'd noticed the clue, and was quite as surprised as I.

"– and it was almost all the way under the shelves, but I'd spotted it all right, and handed it over to that girl, as it hadn't seemed the kind of thing a person should leave lying around."

Of course this interesting little snippet of news threw all of Kimberly's evidence into disarray, as if *April* had picked the Insulin pen from under the shelves, then Kimberly, too, was not telling the truth about the matter and for a terrible moment I thought I might have got it all quite wrong and would need to add Kimberley to the ever-growing list of suspects just when I thought I was on the verge of narrowing down the blessed thing. A sudden chill crawled up my spine and I gave quite the shudder thinking about it, even though as far as I knew Kimberly had not left Book club at any point since she had arrived until after Carrie had called for help. Even then, she hadn't gone immediately and only sometime later when we had wondered if the police had been summoned to the scene, so I simply couldn't see any plausible way that Kimberly could be Charlotte's assassin, however much I racked my brain about it.

"Goodness," I said to no one in particular, "this is all getting most confusing and convoluted. How ever could two people find a medical device under the shelving in the space of one morning? It hardly seems possible and a rather remarkable coincidence."

"Was it Kimberly you gave the pen to?" Mary said, in a timid kind of voice as if she wasn't quite certain about speaking.

Nonetheless, I was terribly grateful she had spoken up, as I hadn't thought about that possibility at all. I gave myself a little internal reprimand for missing something so obvious, but April said goodness, no, she had given it straight to the young librarian, not an ordinary member of the public, so that put that to bed at once. Besides, as Kimberly quickly reminded me, she had picked the pen up *after* Charlotte had died, and April had said Charlotte was there when she had picked up the pen, hadn't she?

"Perhaps Kimberly had not found anything more sinister than a biro after all?" Josephine suggested, and I thought she must be correct.

"I *had* thought that," Kimberly said, "and when I went back and asked Carrie about it afterwards, she said that too. But I did want to be sure, after what Mrs Smith said." She took a little pause, and I imagined she was casting one of those quick little glances at me. "So, I asked Carrie to let me have another look at it, just to check." She took a quick breath and her voice shifted, so I wondered if she had turned her face in another direction and supposed she might be looking towards Carrie now instead, although as far as I was aware, Carrie was not in the room and I thought she might still be in her position at the desk. "I wanted to make sure it wasn't anything special or had anyone's name on it or been anything personal that someone might have dropped. and Carrie rooted under the desk for a bit, but the pen she showed me wasn't the one I found."

"How could you tell?" Phyllis said, which I think you'll agree was a terribly useful question.

"Different colour. The one she gave me was blue, with some logo or the other, and it wasn't remotely the same. I told her, and she faffed about a bit more and said she didn't know where it had gone. I told her Mrs Smith said it might be important. She rolled her eyes a bit, but rooted about a bit more and found the right one, and that's when Ashwini came up and said it looked like an EpiPen and called out to Dougal. I must say Carrie looked quite cross about it all. Said she hadn't known it was one of those, and now she'd have something else to deal with. Poor woman. I'm sure it was the same one, though, because of the colour. I'm sorry I didn't look at it a bit more carefully but I didn't think it was anything important ... just a pen."

I let that roll around in my mind while I tried to think of what it all might mean, but it was quite the muddle and I simply couldn't work it out.

While I was mulling it over, it came to me that April had confirmed a different point entirely, so it seemed a good idea to clear that up whilst we left the other matter to brew for a minute or two. "April, while you were in the meeting room, would you say that you *and* Carrie might have been at the machine contraption, and not visible from the window? Might you have been concealed from the window cleaners by cabinets or shelves and whatnots?"

She said she didn't know about whatnots, but she was tucked away behind the shelving units so she could get at the microfiche machine. She thought about it for a moment, and then agreed that it had been Carrie who had talked her through it all.

"Yes," she said, "we'd have been bent over it, going through the first newspaper clipping together. The senior one – Carrie – walked me through the instructions ... showed me which buttons to press ... where to put the little film things, you know? I guess we were hidden away, all right."

"Where was Charlotte?"

"Standing nearby picking at her nails, face like sucking a lemon. Then off she went in a huff." April didn't hesitate in her answer, and I don't believe she realised how quickly she'd slipped into idle gossip about someone who had just been murdered. I kept that thought to myself, as I didn't want to put her off, not when she was in the throes of sharing some useful clues and suchlike.

"Never one to get her hands dirty, our Charlotte." Barbara gave one of her dry chuckles. "Not that that's any reason to bump her off," she added hastily. "No one deserves *that*. Poor thing."

"It sounds very much as if we have solved another part of the mystery," I said. "I think we can deduce that it must have been Carrie and April the window cleaners couldn't see, when they spotted Charlotte in the meeting room, don't you agree?" I offered the question to the room in general, and everyone seemed to concur.

"As a matter of clarity," I said next, "what colour *is* your insulin device, Isobel?"

"Turquoise."

"The pen I found was turquoise. That's how I knew Carrie had passed me the wrong pen," Kimberley said, her voice heavy and dull. I supposed she had decided that Isobel was undoubtedly responsible for Charlotte's death, and that she herself had held the weapon in her hands. I expect she was terribly afraid that Finbury would charge her with aiding and abetting or that kind of thing, although I didn't suppose he had the sense to think of anything like that, if you ask me.

"I found a turquoise one, too," April said. "Do you have these things all over the place? Is diabetes a common disease over here? There's sure a lot of diabetes back home, these days ..." She trailed off, and I wondered if she was one of those Americans who eat a tower of syrup-coated pancakes stacked up like the leaning tower of Pisa for breakfast every day. I immediately gave myself a little mental shake and reminded myself that of course most Americans were perfectly ordinary and probably just had a bowl of cornflakes or a slice of toast. After all, I was perfectly certain that most people in Little Wittering didn't partake of a full English fried breakfast every day. April hadn't sounded at all heavy when she'd sat down at the table a few minutes ago. Of course, one can't tell for sure when one can't see a person, but one can get an impression, nonetheless.

From the end of the table where Isobel and Mary sat, there came the faintest, sporadic tap-tapping of someone using one of those clever little touchscreen phones my son has explained to me, and knocking the screen with a fingernail from time to time, and Mary said, "Five-point-eight million and going up."

Joan said, "Goodness, that's an awfully large number," and Josephine said, "How many people are in the UK nowadays?" and Mary said, "Hang on," and then, a moment after, "Ah. Sixty-eight million. Blimey. That's loads."

"What's that as a percentage, then?" Barbara said, and Mary said, "Hang on," again, and I supposed she was tapping away a bit more, although I couldn't discern any kind of tapping, but then she said, "'bout eight-point-five percent. So ..."

"Give's a bit of your paper, Phyl." There was a *shhh* on the table beside me, and Barbara said, "Ta," so I supposed Phyl might have shoved her notebook across the table, and then there was the soft bumbling of a pen on paper and Barbara listed names out loud, whilst I supposed she simultaneously scribbled them onto the page. "Joan, Sal, Phyllis, Kim, Bel, Mares, Jo, me, Ash ... Carrie, Charlotte ... American, what's your name again?"

"Um ... April."

"Ta. The two geezers at the computers ... is that it? Thirteen of us ... What's eight point five of that, then?"

"One point one," Mary said and I must say I was terribly impressed at how quickly she solved that little mathematical challenge, as I wouldn't have expected her to be the type, which just goes to show that anyone can be good at maths even if they are more predisposed to the study of English Literature.

"Likely not to be more than one of use here, then," Isobel said quietly. "Looks like you've all made up your minds. It wasn't me, though. And, yeah, my pen isn't here, is it." Her voice had a bitter, resigned edge, and I felt quite sorry for her. "I guess none of you have thought about what'll happen now if I need my insulin, if I've dumped it all into someone else. Ever seen anyone go into a diabetic coma, have you? Think it's a risk I'd take?"

I had to admit that she had a very good point. I simply couldn't imagine that anyone who had such a condition and knew the dangers would willingly compromise their own life-saving medication. I wondered if it be one of those funny little red herrings one finds in Agatha Christie's novels, but I hadn't much time to think about it, as somewhere to the front of the library, a siren wailed to a stop. A moment later, there was a firm, authoritative tapping at the library door, so I supposed someone was knocking to be let in.

Sure enough, not a moment later, Carrie's practical shoes clopped a few steps across the laminate floor, and the door swooshed open.

All at once, a sensible-sounding female voice said, "Hello Carrie, sorry about all this. Where is he then?"

I couldn't be entirely certain, but I thought it might be the reassuring voice of D.S. Sana Nasir, who is senior to Finbury and infinitely more competent and pleasant. D.S. Nasir is a prime example of what one would hope for from the Great British constabulary.

Carrie gave a bit of a sigh and said, "Hello Sana, you'd better come in," which rather proved me right.

Chapter Sixteen

Detective Sergeant Sana Nasir immediately took control of the situation. After a minute or two getting the details from Carrie, she could be heard quite clearly asking Finbury to relay exactly what he'd ascertained thus far, and once he began to get into it, she made the odd little noise of agreement, but on the whole, she said little. When he had finished, she said she thought it might be useful if she had a little look around, and make herself known to the people in the library.

"I'll take it from there," she said, in her no-nonsense manner. "Perhaps the best thing you could do, Constable, is to call the hospital and see if they have any more information about Miss Lewisham. Suggest they check for an overdose of insulin if they could."

Of course, he said, "Yes ma'am," in the kind of voice a petulant child might use, and I wouldn't have been at all surprised if anyone had told me he was pouting like a carp with some of that fashionable Botox whatnot.

I supposed the D.S. didn't wait around for him to argue, as there was the sound of a pair of her very sensible police-officer shoes clip-clopping towards us. "Hello ladies, I'm D.S. Nasir. I'm sure P.C. Finbury has already talked to some of you but if you wouldn't mind staying put, I might need another word with one or two of you in a moment or two," and then she gave a tiny gasp and said, "Oh hello, Sally. Good, you're here."

I had quite the moment of pleasure that she had remembered my name, as we had not met very often and I wouldn't say we knew each other at all well, but nonetheless, it is gratifying to be remembered in a favourable manner. You won't be at all surprised to know that my response to her arrival echoed her sentiments entirely, so I replied at once with, "D.S. Nasir. Good, you're here," which made her laugh in most pleasant way. All at once I felt entirely certain the matter would soon be dealt with in a most efficient and indisputable resolution, and we would all be able to get on with our day.

"I will speak to you in just a moment, Sally, but first, I have a few questions to put to everyone, so it's convenient to find so many of you gathered in one place. Bear with me while I get the others. We may as well confer around this table. Stay where you are, everyone, please."

Her footsteps faded across the library. As she approached the desk, she directed Carrie to join us, speaking in her calm, clear, sensible voice. "And you two gentlemen," she called a moment later, so I supposed she had spotted Gary and Harry. "Please join us in the meeting room. Thank you. Is anyone else here, Carrie?"

Carrie said no, not in the building, as far as she knew. Then she gave one of those little snorts, and added, "Well, your constable, but you know that already," and her tone of voice left us in no doubt whatsoever as to how much use she felt he might bring to the situation.

D.S. Nasir said, "Quite," in an equally dry tone, and after a few seconds, there was the sound of four sets of feet approaching the meeting room, and the scraping of chairs and a bit of muttering about who should sit where and people shifting about to get settled. Once the room fell silent, the Detective Sergeant said, "Now then, it seems the first thing to determine is whether anyone amongst us is diabetic. I don't believe P.C. Finbury has established that yet?" and Isobel said in a somewhat mutinous tone, "Me."

There was one of those silences that one might describe in the clichéd pin-drop kind of way, had it not been for Doofus Finbury loudly addressing someone in the hospital on his telephone in the other room, and the birds twittering cheerfully beyond the window.

"And, yes," Isobel added when no one else spoke, "my insulin appears to be missing. And no, I didn't stab it into Charlotte, because I'm not a complete idiot, am I?"

The D.S. asked Isobel if she wouldn't mind giving her name, and Isobel did so, and the D.S. said thank you, and then she immediately moved on.

I knew at once that she was keeping an open mind about things and not jumping to any hasty conclusions in the incompetent way Dougal Rufus Finbury tended to do, which was terribly reassuring and balanced of her, don't you agree?

The D.S. quickly went through some other points, which I supposed might help her make head or tail of whatever garbled information she'd managed to get out of Finbury. To be perfectly honest, I wondered if she mightn't be better off to start from scratch. Nonetheless, she made to best of it, and I imagined she was checking her notes in a terribly careful and organised manner, as she is an awfully thorough and meticulous kind of police officer. She asked a few quite general questions to us all, such as who had spoken to Charlotte, and who had gone with her anywhere other than the main desk, and if there was anyone present who might have seen or heard anything that may be useful to the inquiry. D.S. Nasir gathered our responses in the same sensible manner as that with which she asked them. I suspected she was recording meticulous notes into one of those smartphones or suchlike, as there was only the occasional faint tap and none of the scratching one would associate with taking notes by hand into a notebook. I imagine someone in her position must be quite *au fait* with all the modern technology, wouldn't you agree?

"All right," she said, after about ten minutes or so. "That gives me a good start. Thank you. I just have a couple more questions, and then we can see who can leave and who might still need to give a statement."

"Detective Sergeant," I said, when she came to a break in the proceedings. "Something you may find of particular interest is that we may have more than one of those insulin pens to think about, and you may find it useful to establish whether there are, in fact, more than one of them about the place. If that is not the case, you see, it seems most likely that some people have been mistaken in their accounts. Or," I said as a thought struck me, "whether several people handled the *same* device."

Of course, she was very interested in this, and asked for a little more clarification on the matter. Several people started to speak at once, and D.S. Nasir said, "Okay, let's take this one at a time. Perhaps this is something I should speak to people individually about, so why don't we start with you, Isobel, as we can be quite certain that you, at least, had an insulin pen in your possession today? Is that all right with you?"

Isobel could hardly argue, but she did ask in a most subdued tone whether she was under arrest. "I didn't kill her, I really didn't, and I don't know where my insulin is." Her voice became terribly trembly, and I'm quite sure she was awfully worried. She asked the detective sergeant if she could call her mum to bring her another one as she didn't like to be without it, and I had quite the wave of sympathy wash over me, as she really is terribly young. I suppose it was the worry of what she might do if she had need of the insulin that set her off, as she began to cry again.

There was a bit of shuffling and some of those murmured platitudes one offers when faced with someone in distress, and then D.S. Nasir said Isobel should go with her to a more private place to have a proper chat, and they'd go via the lavatories to find her a tissue and compose herself.

Someone's chair rubbed across the carpet, so I suppose Isobel was getting herself up.

D.S. Nasir said she would commandeer the space over near the computers, if that was all right with Carrie, as that seemed to offer the most privacy now everyone else was gathered in the meeting room.

"Yes," Carrie said, in her usual perfunctory manner. "That's probably the best place."

Josephine asked whether the D.S. would like a cup of tea, and the D.S. said why not, so up got Josephine too, and off they all went, with D.S. Nasir and Isobel passing behind my chair on their way to the lavatories, and Josephine clumping around the table to wherever it was she had found to plug in the kettle.

Phyllis leant close enough to my ear that I could feel her breath lift my hair a little. "Ha!" she whispered as softly as a summer breeze. "She said she wasn't going to make any more tea." I gave her a little swat with my hand, and she added in her normal voice that perhaps Josephine would make sure there was water enough for us to have a hot cup after all, since we hadn't managed it before.

Josephine muttered something quite rude, but judging by the clanking and clunking, I deduced she must be taking up the kettle, and then she clomped off after the D.S. on her heavy feet, so I supposed she was off to fill it with water and I guessed she would do as Phyl had suggested with only a little grumbling.

As soon as the Detective Sergeant had led away poor, sobbing Isobel, and Josephine had gone after them with the kettle, the wave of chatter took up again around our meeting room table. I must say that the most evident feeling was one was one of relief that the D.S. had arrived, with her air of capability and common sense. Once everyone had made some comment about that, most of us expressed some concern about Isobel. Some were of the opinion that she had indeed done the deed, although others amongst us were not at all sure that was the case. Nonetheless, we were in perfect agreement that we all felt terribly worried for the poor girl.

"The thing is," the American voice spoke up, a little way around the table to my right, "I got that pen up off the floor and gave it to the younger librarian – Charlotte, right? – so don't you see, if the pen is that poor little girl's pen, as she seems to think it is, that must mean that she didn't have it, because I had already given it to the librarian to deal with, don't you see? The librarian appeared to be well and in good health, as far as I could see, and she took it from me and said something along the lines of thanks, and she was very much *alive*."

"And if Charlotte already had the insulin, Isobel can't have injected it into her?"

"Could she have done it first, and dropped the thing, and it not have taken any affect yet?"

"Shouldn't think so. I think it acts fast enough, doesn't it?"

"Hang on ... I'll look it up," Mary said, and this time, she must have been typing the instruction into her telephone more frantically, as one could most certainly make out the thudding of her fingers on the screen, so I expect she was jabbing at it quite furiously. "Seems like it would've had some effect immediately ... she'd have keeled over pretty much on the spot, looks like ... Ashwini?"

"I am already asking the doctor. I'm sure he will respond in a minute or two, if he is not too busy." I imagined her to be holding up her own telephone and waving it about in the way one brandishes a trophy, but of course she could just as easily have been sending her husband a discreet message typed beneath the table, for all I knew.

"April," I said, as everyone else fell silent to await Dr Patil's reply, "what did Charlotte do with the pen?"

She said she didn't know, and then one of the men said, "I do."

"Who is that?" I said, as I couldn't discern whether it had been Gary or Harry, and several voices answered at the same time to say it was Harry, and then he said, "She took it to the desk and gave it to Carrie."

Chapter Seventeen

As soon as Harry said that, a great many things fell into place at once. Consequently, I was immediately certain as to who had killed Charlotte, and how they had done it. We had already established the reasons for it, so that was by the by. I fumbled about for Phyllis, and patted her sharply on the arm. Once I had her attention, I said it might be a very good idea if I could speak with the Detective Sergeant, but she was not to worry about taking me, as she had already done quite the to-ing and fro-ing bringing me about. "Amity and I will manage perfectly well," I said. I pushed back my chair and got to my feet, and as I did so, I made a great pretence of stumbling towards my dear friend, putting out my hands in order to decipher exactly whereabouts her ear might be. As soon as I had it located, I leaned in close and whispered, "Don't let anyone leave."

Phyllis said, "All right Sally, if you are sure. I am a little wobbly on my feet after all the excitement, so I will stay here with everyone if you don't mind, and perhaps Carrie or Barbara or someone might pass around that biscuit tin to give us all a little boost."

I knew from her response that she had heard my whisper and was onto it. If I knew Phyllis half as well as I thought I did, she would not let a single person move from the room, so I could be quite certain the perpetrator wouldn't get away.

With that, Amity took me very carefully and precisely across the floor to the Detective Sergeant, whom I could hear quite clearly speaking to Isobel. Isobel seemed to have stopped crying and was explaining quite calmly how to see if the insulin from the pen had been used or not, so I was glad that the D.S. had seen some sense. I guessed she was probably already along the same track as I was about it, and had realised immediately that Isobel was off the hook, as they say.

"Where do you think you are off to then?" A whiff of bacon breath smacked me in the face as a large, buffoon-shaped shadow stepped into my path. Had it not been for Amity's quick-thinking, I might have fallen flat onto my face. As it was, she swerved me abruptly to one side, whilst emitting a low, warning growl in the direction of the odious shadow.

"Dougal Rufus," I said in the firmest voice I could summon, "I have some information I need to share with your superior, and if you could kindly step out of my way, I will continue towards her."

"She's busy."

"I am very much of the mind that she will want to hear what it is I have to share, and will be significantly less busy if she takes a moment to listen to what I have concluded. Do move aside before Amity chews a hole in your leg. She believes you are a threat to my safety and she is trained to protect me, you see."

"Mrs Smith! I forbid you to interrupt a police officer in the middle of an investigation!"

Amity's growl became a little louder, imparting a little more menace into her tone, even though she is a perfect dear and would never have such bad manners as to snap at a person without my permission, even if that person were a bacon-scented idiot.

As you will have guessed, I had ensured that the exchange between myself and the abhorrent Finbury had been executed as clearly and loudly as possible. I could not, of course, instigate any clarity into his words, but the volume was entirely predictable. Sure enough, from the vicinity of the computer section, Detective Sergeant Nasir said, "Excuse me for just a minute, Isobel."

The clop of sturdy shoes on laminate assured me of her approach. Sure enough, mere seconds passed before D.S. Nasir said, "Come on over, Mrs Smith. I have just about finished with Isobel. I'm very interested to hear what you have noticed."

Finbury huffed and harrumphed and said how could I have noticed anything when I couldn't *see*, which was just about what one might expect from him.

"You would be surprised what a person might notice if they are paying attention." D.S. Nasir spoke in quite the tone of voice that might suggest Finbury was *not* the kind of person who paid attention.

He didn't say anything in response, but I expect he might have turned a rather unbecoming shade of puce, much as he used to when asked if he could possibly try to complete his homework *without* the help from his pet hamster.

"Oh dear," I said, as D.S. Nasir offered me her arm and guided my hand into the crook of her elbow. "It must be terribly difficult being his superior. I was his teacher, you know."

She gave a sigh of perfect understanding. I felt at once as if she and I were the colleagues working together to solve the crime, and Finbury the most unhelpful of witnesses, quite unable to see past the nose on his face.

"Goodness," I said, as she guided me to one of those uncomfortable plastic chairs in the computer section. "He really is quite the challenge. If only I had done better as his teacher, perhaps he would have become entirely more observant. One does sometimes wish one had tried harder, you know? Now, where will I start? Isobel, dear, are you still here? If the Detective Sergeant agrees, perhaps you'd be kind enough to see if that tea is ready. I suggest you ask Josephine."

I am quite sure D.S. Nasir realised at once that I wished Isobel to leave us to it, because she said, yes, she would appreciate that very much, as it was incredibly hot, wasn't it? She didn't know how we'd all sat in the library all morning, and wondered why we hadn't thought about sitting outside for our meetings. "Have you not considered sitting in the park on a day as lovely as this?" she went on, and I supposed she was just passing the time with some pleasantries until Isobel was out of earshot.

Of course, I played along, and told her that there would be little point in arranging it, as we could be quite certain that if we took it upon ourselves to schedule the meetings for the park, it would rain.

The D.S. laughed and said she supposed it would, and then I deduced that Isobel must have got herself out of the way, as her voice lowered and became altogether more serious: "So, Sally, I suppose you are going to tell me that Isobel couldn't possibly have harmed Charlotte, and then you will present a reasonably conclusive argument as to why it was someone else, and I will almost certainly agree with your theory and make an arrest?"

I said, yes, I rather thought that might be the case.

"Hmm," she said, as if she were thinking it over for a minute, and then she said she might even let P.C. Finbury do the arrest, as it would make him feel important and useful. Neither of us were so unprofessional as to voice the opinion, but I can be fairly certain she thought the same as I, which was that he would never be particularly important or useful, which is terribly unkind, but I'm very much afraid it is probably true.

I brushed away the thought, and explained how I had quickly come to suspect both Isobel and Harry, and how Phyllis had added Carrie to the mix. "Then, during P.C. Finbury's interrogations, I had to add Gary to the list, although I was terribly reluctant about it. You mustn't think I was eavesdropping." I was quick to reassure the Detective Sergeant about that as I didn't want her mistaking me for the kind of person who listens to another's private conversations. "But he can be terribly *loud*."

"Indeed. It would be difficult *not* to overhear."

"I'm afraid it would," I said with the kind of sigh that conveys a balance of sorrow and hopelessness in the face of having tried one's best in a difficult situation such as being the teacher of such an unfortunate case as Dougal Rufus Finbury. "I simply couldn't fathom out any kind of motive for Isobel to have done the deed, despite my suspicions as to her behaviour during the morning. I wasn't entirely certain as to whether she even knew Charlotte very well. Isobel, you see, is quite new to our book club, and I can't say I have managed to get to know her very well just yet. Harry, on the other hand, seemed to be quite infatuated by Charlotte, by all accounts. Despite that, I had good reasons to suspect him from the very moment I realised Charlotte was dead."

"Why?"

I relayed the conversation I had overheard in the lavatories at approximately five minutes to ten that morning. I could be perfectly accurate with the approximate time, I said, if that were not a contradiction in terms, because it was not long after Phyllis and I had arrived at the library, and a few minutes before the book club meeting got started.

"We like to start at ten," I said, "so everyone is present by five to, usually. I left my house in Florence Court at nine-fifteen and collected Phyllis at the corner. We stopped to let Amity have a bit of a run, and then got on our way. We arrived before the other ladies, as we usually do, so we can do our other library business before we settle down to the book club. I would estimate our arrival to have been no later than quarter-to, wouldn't you think? Phyllis had a bit of a wander about in the book shelves and we both chatted to Carrie and the American. Phyllis had plenty of time to choose her new books before the next of our group arrived, and that was Joan and Barbara. Phyl is usually very quick with her choices, as she comes with a list. She does like to have a list; she's terribly organised. We were both chatting at the counter when Barbara and Joan came in. Carrie had nipped out with Jeff, so Phyl and I were about to move on when they entered. Phyl and Joan and Barbara all went off to the meeting room, and Amity and I went to the Ladies' room. Are you managing to get all this down?"

D.S. Nasir said yes, she was managing it quite well, so I continued.

"It was the conversation overheard in the Ladies, you see, that was the first clue that Charlotte's death may have been neither accidental or natural. Of course, I hadn't realised it at the time, because of course she wasn't dead at that point in the proceedings."

"No, I suppose she wasn't," D.S. Nasir said with one of those abrupt sounds one makes when one almost laughs in an inopportune moment and manages to stop it just in time.

"In point of fact, I only started to think about it being a clue after I heard the second clue, so perhaps the second was the first, now I came to think about it, but the order hardly seemed to matter at the time."

"Go on."

"Charlotte was quite animated during her telephone conversation, and although I couldn't hear all she said, what with trying not to eavesdrop, and the certain other noises one would expect to hear in a public lavatory such as flushing and running water and the hand dryer and whatnot, so I'm sure you'll understand that some of what she said was somewhat fragmented."

"Why don't you tell me what you can recall, Sally, and I will attempt to put it together, and then we can see if we have reached similar conclusions?" D.S. Nasir said, which was a very sensible approach to take, if you ask me.

"She was talking about a man who had been causing her quite some bother. She was quite distressed about it. Not in a crying kind of way, but in that high-pitched way one gets into when one is getting worked up about something. I got quite the impression that the man in question had been visiting her in the library whenever he had the opportunity. She said he wouldn't leave her alone and she was quite fed up with it. She didn't say explicitly, but I had the impression they had been boyfriend and girlfriend for some time, but she had put an end to it. He didn't seem to have taken much notice of that decision, which seemed to be the root of the problem. 'Won't take no,' she said to whomever it was she was speaking with, and she sounded quite cross about it, which one can understand, of course. She said she'd asked Carrie to get him to leave. Then she said Carrie had said she couldn't ban someone just for looking at her strangely, and that was about the time I flushed the lavatory, so I didn't get much of what she said next, except the odd snippet about someone always watching her to see what she was at, and looking at her like they'd kill her. I presumed she was still talking about the young man, but after I'd spoken to Phyllis about it, I realised I couldn't be sure about that. Are you following me without too much difficulty? It is rather convoluted, I'm afraid. I do so wish I had been able to write it all down as I'm sure I could have got it together in a more sensible manner."

You won't be at all surprised to know that the Detective Sergeant was most reassuring. "You're doing very well, Sally. Do keep going, if you don't mind."

I continued to relay my account, and told her that later on, during our book club meeting, someone had mentioned a handsome young man over by the computers. Isobel had been quite swoony about him, and that had started some of the others off. "Then Mary said she had seen him talking to Charlotte, and from the little snippets I managed to put together from that, I deduced quite easily that he must have been the same man Charlotte had been telling her friend about." I stopped for a moment to gather my thoughts and work out exactly where I was getting to.

"Go on, when you're ready."

I imagined the D.S. to be nodding her head, or perhaps peering at her notebook or little screen or whatnot, but of course she may have been gazing out of the window of across the library or simply wondering about that cup of tea, but I expect she was paying perfectly good attention, nonetheless.

"That young man named Harry." I said, by way of clarification. "He's in the meeting room with the others, probably causing quite a stir amongst the ladies. They all seem to be in perfect agreement that he is perfectly handsome, even though some of them have their minds made up that he is also a cold-blooded killer. Even those who are keeping an open mind about it or suspect it mightn't have been him at all are in agreement that he was causing Charlotte quite the bother. He was indisputably the type of person to inflict himself upon someone even after they have made it entirely clear his attentions are unwanted, which doesn't say a lot for his character, if you ask me. However, whilst Charlotte was perturbed about being watched, after I thought about it, I realised it seemed awfully likely she was irritated by not *one* person, but by *two*."

D.S. Nasir continued to listen in that attentive manner of one who only interjects only for point of clarification or to say, "Go on," from time to time.

"The second clues," I went on, "were given by Isobel." Isobel, I informed the D.S., had seemed to know that Charlotte had been attacked before anyone had said so, although it is possible it was a slip of the tongue and not any kind of certain knowledge, one must suppose. "I imagine a person may sometimes say 'she' or 'he' when they don't have any real knowledge as to whom they refer, but she also lied about having left the room, and was a little agitated upon her return, and more so again at hearing that it was, indeed, Charlotte, who had died. It is a perfectly logical deduction to presume Isobel knew exactly who was dead because she was the one who had killed her, don't you agree?"

D.S. Nasir said, yes, she could see at once how one might think such a thing.

I explained how it had become quite apparent that Isobel was very much hankering after that young man. She had admitted to us all that if only Charlotte was out of the way, perhaps he'd pay some attention to her, so of course that had pricked up my ears at once. "Gary reiterated that point when Phyl and I were having a little chat with him. He said Isobel had been gazing most wistfully after Harry for weeks, but Harry hadn't even noticed her."

"I see. Go on, Sally, please. This is all very interesting."

Joan, I told the D.S., had it spot on when she had suggested Isobel had, indeed, intended to go to the lavatories, but become distracted by Harry appearing at just that moment. Isobel had already admitted that instead of going into the Ladies, she had followed Harry across the room, thinking he might be going outside and perhaps hoping for a chance to speak to him. She would certainly know he is a smoker, if she has been drooling after him for some time, wouldn't you think?"

"It seems likely."

"Besides, I can confirm it quite easily. One can distinctly discern the smell of that tobacco one likes to roll into a little cigarette, if one stands close enough to the boy. It's not unpleasant," I said to the D.S., "or at all over-powering, so I don't believe he is a heavy smoker. Perhaps the type who likes to emulate James Dean or some such idol, I shouldn't wonder, and hangs a cigarette from a nonchalant kind of sneer without actually smoking the thing, if that is possible nowadays?"

She said she thought it might be, and she knew the kind of look I meant, which shows that she is perfectly able to visualise a clue, don't you agree?

"I noticed when Isobel returned to the meeting room, she smelled of the same kind of cigarettes. However, when we asked her about it later, it seems she procured one from the window cleaner, so that, I'm afraid, seems to be a mere coincidence. I'm sure you'll agree that it is quite common for more than one person to smoke the same kind of cigarettes, when one has a somewhat limited choice. After all, one would hardly make an arrest based on a person drinking the same brand of supermarket coffee as another, would one?"

She said no, that would not be enough at all, and her partner liked the same kind of roll-ups, too, although she didn't smoke herself, but one puts up with some things. She gave a little sigh at that, so I supposed she was wondering about how much is reasonable to put up with, in a relationship.

I told her Dennis and I had been married for decades, and he had one or two most unpleasant habits, but overall, he is very good, and would probably say the same about me, if one gave him the chance.

She said, yes, she supposed so, and asked me what else had I noticed, which was probably her clever little way of getting me back on track, wouldn't you agree?

Chapter Eighteen

I took a moment to gather my thoughts and see where it was I had got to. "Well, by then, Phyllis and some of the others had quite surprised me with the information that Carrie had not, as I had thought, got over the promotion. It seems she has been displaying quite the air of disapproval towards Charlotte. I'm terribly sorry that I had been entirely unaware of the fact. Once I stated to think about it, I realised at once that Carrie had simply pretended she didn't mind about the promotion because if there is one thing one can agree on about Carrie, it is that she is terribly professional and efficient."

"Two things, then."

We had a little chuckle about that and I said I could add a few points more, too, but nothing of any pertinence to the matter. "Suffice to say, Carrie *is* hard-working and diligent, and Charlotte, it seems, was not. Many people have corroborated that fact through the morning, so it was not unnoticed."

"Yes," said the D.S., so I suppose she agreed about that.

"Many have also confirmed Phyllis's observation that Carrie, it seemed, had a great distaste for her younger colleague, so when I took some to think about it, I wondered if it had been *Carrie* to whom the second part of Charlotte's telephone conversation referred. After I had flushed the lavatory, that is. It got me thinking that perhaps it had been *Carrie* who had been looking at Charlotte in such a way as make her worry. She had, after all, already described Harry's incessant gaze as puppy-dog, sickly, and irritating, but not, at any point, in words one associates with danger. *After* the gurgling of the flushing had abated, Charlotte was talking about 'looks that could kill' and 'shooting daggers', so with the benefit of digesting other people's observations, she could very well have been talking about two entirely different people, don't you think?"

"Hmm," D.S. Nasir said, so she seemed to be giving it some consideration. "Not Isobel? She'd have reason as much as Carrie, to, er, shoot daggers, wouldn't you say?"

"I did consider that, of course," I said, "and I must admit it is a possibility, but then Isobel told us that Charlotte had told her she was welcome to pursue Harry, and that they'd had a little chat, and cleared the air about it. Of course, it was only after Phyllis suggested Carrie might wish Charlotte out of the way in revenge for the promotion, that I started to put those clues together and added her to the list of suspects, but once Phyllis had opened my eyes about that, so to say, it fell into place terribly neatly. It seems altogether more likely, given the evidence about it all, that it was Carrie giving the daggers, don't you agree? Or possibly Isobel, but not Harry, one shouldn't think."

I hadn't heard any new tapping or anything like a pen scratching or a pen grumbling over a notepad, so I wasn't entirely certain as to whether D.S. Nasir was taking any notes about it, but perhaps she was just listening and taking it all in.

I suspect she is the kind of person who would know what she should write down or not. Finbury, by contrast, is barely the kind of person who can write his own name, but that is by the by.

"So you see, although the evidence and opportunity appeared to favour poor Isobel, she didn't appear to have a particularly strong motive, aside from clearing the path to Harry's attentions, which was in no way guaranteed. Indeed, with clarity of thought, he would appear to be the type to wallow in grief at losing the object of his infatuation, and therefore pay even *less* attention to a person he had not noticed at all so far. But of course, one doesn't think about such things when one is young and in love, so I don't suppose Isobel would have considered that." I paused for moment to think about it, and Detective Sergeant Nasir took the opportunity to say, "Mm-hm," and then after a moment, "Maybe not. Do go on."

"The problem," I said, "is that both Gary and April both saw Isobel and Harry talking with Charlotte in the non-fiction area shortly before her death was discovered, and that is terribly unfortunate for them both."

"And for Charlotte."

"Precisely."

"Who exactly was it who discovered her?"

"Carrie, as far as I know. I believe she spotted her there and immediately called for help although I suppose you will need to clarify that to be sure. Ashwini went at once, as she knows a bit about it, what with being married to Doctor Patil for all those years. He's a terribly good doctor. It must rub off a bit, wouldn't you agree?"

"I suppose it would."

"By the time Ashwini got there, the two men were there too. She said Harry was just sitting there with his head in his hands, and Gary was trying to administer some level of first aid, but didn't really know what he was doing."

"Why do you think it was that the two men were the first ones there? Does that strike you as suspicious?"

I had a little think about that and said I thought not, as the computer section was adjacent to the non-fiction, so they would have been closest. "You could ask the American how it was she didn't see anything, as I would have thought she would have had a view of the whole situation, if she were still at the microfiche, now I have been informed it has been moved into the meeting room."

The Detective Sergeant was quiet for a moment and there was a faint noise as if she might be typing something, so I supposed she might be making a note of it, but then she said, "Actually, if someone is tucked in that little alcove where the microfiche is, they would be behind the wall."

I was somewhat confused by this, as I was of the impression that the corrugated divider opened the full width of the meeting room, and D.S. Nasir said, "Wait just a moment." Her chair rubbed on the carpet; the air shifted a little, and a shadow moved across the light from the window, so I supposed she had risen from her seat.

Sure enough, seconds later, the movements replayed in reverse order – a shadow, a swoosh of air, a chair shuffling towards the table as she sat again. "No, it is as I thought, Sally. There is about four feet of solid wall joining on to the outside wall, to each side of the library. I imagine it is needed to support the roof, but I wouldn't know enough about buildings ... There are three separate corrugated walls. One to divide the two meeting rooms, so they can be made into one large meeting room, and one to divide each of the meeting rooms from the main library. There is another bit of solid wall where all three meet, almost like a pillar, but T-shaped. The microfiche is against the protruding piece of wall that joins onto the external wall, so anyone behind it would certainly not be able to see the exact part of the library where Charlotte died, unfortunately. It would appear that she was killed in the section most unlikely to be overlooked, as there is a similar four-foot-long section of wall between where we now sit and the non-fiction section of book shelves. Charlotte was found in the section of shelving that runs perpendicular to the two sections. Do you follow?"

I said I thought I did, although I had quite forgotten that there was any solid wall by the corrugated part, and did she mean right up at the end where the final row of books is mounted to the external wall, and she said yes. I said, I think that used to be where the art and photography books were kept as they were often oversized and heavier, and she said she didn't know about that, and I said Phyllis had said she thought it was cookery and gardening nowadays, so perhaps the art books had been moved to somewhere else.

D.S. Nasir said she didn't know about that either, but perhaps they were opposite one another.

I said yes maybe that was the case, and that it probably wasn't of any great importance as it seemed the location had been selected for being somewhat tucked away, rather than for its reading matter.

She said either way, it was a long section, and seemed to contain a lot of books, and I said Phyllis would know as she used to be the librarian here.

Before we could get any further, Doofus squelched over with his squeaky shoes and asked in his usual bombastic manner if the D.S. had finished with me yet.

"I have spoken to the hospital," he said.

D.S. Nasir said she'd be with him in a minute or two, and perhaps he could check what kinds of books were in the section in which Charlotte had died, and I must confess I had a little inward smile at that as we had just agreed it was of no importance. I immediately concluded she was simply keeping him out of the way, and as soon as he took his squeaky shoes off towards the gardening books, she said in a low voice, "You said you had another suspect? Gary, wasn't it?"

"Yes. Apparently, Charlotte had encouraged his wife to leave him. I could see how that might cause some degree of upset, but as far as I am aware, Gary is terribly pleasant and is the kind of man who gets on with things. He's in here all the time trying to find work, but he's always perfectly cheerful and willing. Barbara knows him quite well. She said Charlotte had helped his wife with finding somewhere to live, but Gary hadn't mentioned anything about that at all, and I hadn't been at all aware they had been having any kind of problems, but I suppose one never knows, does one?"

"Hmm." There came the faint clicks one makes when one's fingernail strike a telephone screen, so I was quite certain she was tapping into her phone or one of those other electronic devices.

I waited a moment or two until I couldn't hear the sounds and she seemed to have finished whatever it was she was tapping into her contraption, and then I went on. "When one thinks about it, there is one person in the library who would have been quite aware of all these factors, and perfectly placed to use it to their advantage. Someone who has time on their hands and sees who comes and goes, and would notice things about their lives, don't you think?"

"Harry?"

"Goodness no. By all accounts, he only had eyes for Charlotte, so he'd hardly have paid attention to anyone else, or cared a jot about it. *Carrie.* She sees everyone who comes into the library and knows an awfully large amount about everyone's business, don't you think? I'm quite certain she had been helping Gary with his job search, for example, and I think we can assume she might have known all about his situation. I would imagine she might have been aware that Charlotte had helped his wife. She is not the type of woman to *miss* anything. It's been perfectly well-established that Charlotte does as little as is humanly possible. Therefore, one must suppose Carrie to have noticed the unusual activity of Charlotte helping someone with something, or that Carrie might have been dragged into it and helped with Jane's getaway or whatnot. Jane is Gary's wife, but I expect you are quite aware of that fact already?"

The D.S. said yes, she was, and to go on with my ideas.

"We must also consider the information that Carrie did nothing to stop Harry harassing Charlotte, even though Gary informed Phyllis and I that Charlotte had asked her on more than one occasion. I also heard Charlotte say the same, when

I overheard her in the lavatories, as I'm sure you noted in that little electronic device of yours. Now I have been made fully aware of Carrie's animosity towards her colleague – the usurper, Phyllis called her, and I must say it seemed to be quite the accurate description, don't you agree? – I wonder if Carrie might have got quite the satisfaction out of Charlotte's discomfort?"

"Mm-hmm." The Detective Sergeant really was a most attentive listener, and I had no doubt she was putting together all the pieces and would soon reach the same conclusions as had I, and see immediately that the correct person was held accountable for poor Charlotte's death.

"Carrie, of course, from her viewpoint behind the desk and beetling about in the library, would undoubtedly have also observed Isobel's behaviour. I think it is a perfectly safe suggestion that Carrie might have noticed Isobel following Harry around like a dog while Harry was doing the same to poor Charlotte, don't you? Carrie is terribly diligent, and would be certain to pay attention to whatever anyone might be up to in the library at any time. She is remarkably quick to sense danger, and has had to leap into action on more than one occasion to stop an incident in the Children's section."

"Mm-hmm."

"So, we can also deduce that she has her wits about her well enough to spot a series of opportunities."

"Go on, Sally."

"Are you getting the important parts down on your device? Is it just an ordinary telephone or something altogether cleverer?"

She said it was a tablet, which is a term I find quite ridiculous, but I suppose they are so-named for those Old Testament kind of stones upon which Moses might have written his commandments, and not those miniscule little Paracetamol tablets or whatnots that one has terrible difficulty extracting from the plastic packaging nowadays. "Wasn't it so much more convenient when one's pharmacist dispensed them into a little brown jar?"

"Pardon?"

Of course, then I had to explain what it was I had been thinking about her tablet contraption, and she had quite the little chuckle. She agreed that the jars had been easier, and that some of the plastic packaging was very tricky, so I wondered if we might start up a little campaign about it in the future once the mystery of Charlotte's murder was dealt with, and all that thinking about medicine brought me right back to the matter in hand.

"I am quite certain that there is only the one Insulin pen at play here, and that whilst it seems to belong to Isobel, it also seems unlikely to have been her who used the thing." Isobel, I told D.S. Nasir, told us that she dropped an armful of books she had been passing to Charlotte. "I imagine the actual delivery of the books was happenstance, as Isobel has already told us she was passing the desk at the right moment, and as we have agreed, Carrie would have spotted that Isobel would have been only too happy for the excuse to go over to Harry. Carrie is not a lazy person by any means, but she is certainly resourceful and quick-thinking, and, as I say, not one to miss an opportunity. I don't suppose that at the moment of passing the books to Isobel that Carrie had considered anything more than a way to get those books from the desk to the shelves. However, I *do* think she exploited Isobel's good deed a very short time later, once she realised it might give her a chance to throw the wool over our eyes, as it were."

"How do you mean?"

"It is perfectly possible that Carrie grasped upon an opportunity to kill Charlotte and frame others for the deed."

The D.S. didn't say anything about that, but there was a tiny shift in the light and a fraction of scraping of chair across carpet, so I wondered if she might have stiffened and sat a little more rigidly upon her hard, plastic chair.

"I think if we ask Isobel, she will say she jumped at the chance to the take the books, and get close to Harry, and interrupt his tête-à-tête with Charlotte. I doubt very much, however, that she has considered any notion of that action becoming the first rung in the ladder of Carrie's opportunity. I suspect it highly unlikely that Carrie herself realised or planned it as such, to be perfectly truthful about it."

"Pre-meditated," muttered the D.S.

"Yes, I believe that is exactly the terminology one would use, or more to the point, *not*, as I feel certain it was more a case of an opportunity arising and an opportunity taken.

"Indeed."

"Isobel told us that when she brought the books to Charlotte, she became so flustered she dropped the books and her bag. One might suppose that when one drops one's bag, its contents may spill out, don't you think?"

D.S. Nasir's chair shifted again, just a fraction, and the shadowy figure seated therein swayed and grew. When she spoke, her voice was marginally louder, as if she had leaned a little towards me, so I deduced my comment had caused her a great deal of interest.

I relayed at once how, upon Isobel's return to the meeting room, she was breathless and ditsy and all of a fluster, which I now suspect was due to an embarrassing occurrence – that of dropping her belongings in the presence of Harry.

As I stopped to give the D.S. time to catch up with her notes, the soft patter of tentative footsteps on laminate flooring neared, and I guessed it to be Isobel herself, presumably approaching with those cups of tea. I lowered my voice and hastily whispered the final implications of my observations to the D.S, hoping she would grasp it at once, before Isobel got to us. "I would also suppose she quickly scooped up whatever she immediately saw scattered about herself, and got herself out of there before causing herself any further embarrassment. I imagine it unlikely she stopped to check whether any of her belongings had rolled under the shelves, wouldn't you agree? Is that you, Isobel?"

The soft, hesitant footsteps halted and Isobel said, "Yes. I brought you both a cup of tea. Josephine wasn't sure how you take yours, Detective. She did milk and no sugar and says she hopes it'll do."

Chapter Nineteen

The detective sergeant was most grateful for the tea, and said milk and no sugar would do her very well, thank you. "How about you give your mother that call and ask her to pop down with the spare insulin?" she said to Isobel. "Or I can have P.C. Finbury pop over to the pharmacy and collect one from there."

Of course, Isobel said she couldn't possibly ask the policeman, and D.S. Nasir said of course she could and it would give him something to do. Well, I can tell you that even Isobel had a little giggle about that and I must say that once again I felt a terrible wave of sympathy not only for the poor girl, but also for the D.S., who had to work with Dougal Rufus Finbury and must find it terribly challenging at times.

Of course, I understood that Isobel didn't at all want to deliver the message to Finbury herself and I imagined she might be standing there all of a tremble. I quickly instructed her to put down the cups of tea, telling her I would be most grateful if she would put mine where I could find it.

As the cup clinked onto the tabletop, she said, "Oops," and then said she'd run across to the counter and grab a tissue, so I supposed it was too late to stop the slopping after all. However, it certainly proved my point about the trembling, so I suggested that Finbury might take the instruction about getting the insulin better from the Detective Sergeant.

The D.S. gave one of those little sighs one might easily miss if one were not accustomed to that reaction when Finbury's name came into a conversation. "Yes, you're quite right. Come with me, Isobel, and we can tell him exactly what it is he needs to get for you." She shoved her chair back with a scrape and another little sigh. "Be right back, Sally."

She was right about that too, as not a minute later, she was back at the table, and Finbury was squeak-huffing past the desk. There was the *swssh* of the door, a waft of air, and a distinct sense of everyone about the library breathing a small sigh of relief that Finbury, at least temporarily, was gone. Of course, I must admit I may have imagined the latter to be completely accurate, but I'm sure you will agree it was at least perfectly plausible.

The D.S. told Isobel to pop back to the others, as she hadn't quite finished with me, and off Isobel padded. Her receding footsteps were altogether quicker than those upon which she had approached us a few minutes beforehand, but I suppose that might have been as much to do with carrying the cups of tea as anything so one can't draw any definite conclusions about that.

There was a shift of air and a little *squoosh* as the D.S. shuffled in her seat, and the faint creaking as she settled into position. "Now, where were we?"

I supposed she must have been peering at her tablet whatnot again, as there was the softest clicking of a finger against the edge of screen, which my son and daughter tell me happens when they are swiping at the contraption. It was terribly difficult for me to fathom out why one might want to swipe at a telephone screen, but my daughter took my hand and showed me exactly what it was they mean. She had stroked my fingers across the smooth glass screen of her device in a rapid sweeping motion, telling me what was happening on the display as I did so. Thereafter, I found it altogether clearer and easier from me to visualise, which just goes to show how easy it can be when a person takes a little time to explains something in a suitable manner, don't you think?

"Ah yes," the D.S. said, "Isobel had dropped her bag. She did mention that to me when I was chatting with her."

I was pleased to hear that Isobel had indeed corroborated the story quite well, and wondered if we might have asked her a bit more about it while she was setting down the tea but it was a little late to think of it now. Nevertheless, as I explained to D.S. Nasir, it was quite straightforward to put together the clues from then on, as we had quite the assortment of witness accounts to draw from.

"April," I said, "spotted the insulin pen in the aisle, to where presumably it had rolled. She picked it up, handed it to Charlotte, and proceeded on her way to wherever it was she was off to."

The Detective Sergeant listened without comment as I relayed my doubt that she went wandering into the back shelves to look for Charlotte, because surely if Charlotte were out of sight, April would have simply passed it to Carrie on her way past the desk. "Thus," I said, "we can suppose Charlotte was in close and obvious proximity to April. I expect you will confirm that with April in due course. It follows, you will agree, that if my deductions are correct, we can presume that

Charlotte was no longer cornered in the back with Harry. It seems Isobel's clumsy intervention had broken up that little *tête-à-tête*, at least. Nevertheless, unless the American is not being entirely truthful, we can be sure that Charlotte had hold of the insulin at some time proceeding her death."

"Do you think the American would have any reason to lie?"

I told her I certainly didn't see any reason, but one can never be sure with anyone, especially when one has only met them for the first time that very morning. She had certainly appeared to be genuine, and I'm quite sure Phyllis agreed, and she is a terribly good judge of character. I explained about April looking for her family and whatnot, and how I expected Phyllis might be keen to give her a bit of a hand with that after all the hoohah of the morning, and we'd have to see about that later on.

D.S. Nasir said it sounded like a nice thing to do, and of course I agreed with her and said Phyllis is the kind of person who can be terribly helpful when she puts her mind to it.

The D.S. said, yes, she had that impression of Phyllis, which just goes to show, and then we got back to the subject of April.

I said I supposed the D.S. would need to use her detecting skills and expertise to decide for sure about how trustworthy April might or might not be, as one must agree some things are significantly easier when one can study a person's facial expressions. The D.S. said she was sure I was right about her, but she would make a note to speak to April just in case, and then she asked if I happened to know what Charlotte had done with the insulin contraption after April had passed it over to her.

I don't like to speak ill of anyone, unless they happen to be an incompetent Police Constable with bacon-scented breath, but I'm sure you are quite *au fait* with the expression about exceptions proving a rule, and Finbury, I can assure you is quite the exception. Nonetheless, I had to admit to the Detective Sergeant that, taking into account what everyone had said about Charlotte's character, we could perhaps conclude it was highly likely she had simply passed the insulin over to Carrie to deal with anyway, so April would have just as well to have given it to Carrie in the first place.

"Mm." The D.S. was most non-committal in her response, so you will have to draw your own conclusions as to what she was thinking. "Even though April had told her what the device was?" she said, after a minute or so.

"I should think so," I said, with one of those little sighs one gives when one feels a level of disappointment with a person, albeit one who is dead and one didn't know terribly well. "We have quite enough evidence of her having passed the buck, as they say, on any other occasion she had been asked to do something."

"Yes." D.S. Nasir gave a little sigh of her own.

"For example, April asked Charlotte for help with the microfiche, and Charlotte passed her straight over to Carrie."

"If we take April's account at face value," the D.S. said quietly, much as if she might be reminding herself that we couldn't be entirely sure of such a thing.

"Indeed. If *anyone* is to be taken at face value," I said. "But one simply can't go about presuming everyone is telling falsehoods, or one would never make any progress at all. Besides, I do find it uses up a lot less energy to suppose most people are honest, don't you?" As soon as I had said the words, I gave myself a little shake and had a little chuckle and said that of course in her job, I imagined the very opposite might be the norm. "I suppose you must be predisposed to looking at everyone as if they had stolen the King's gold."

"Quite," she agreed.

"I would imagine that when the majority of the witnesses corroborate an account, one is more inclined to believe it to be true?" I didn't wait for her to respond, as I had a good deal of evidence to support the idea. "Gary, for example, said he had asked Charlotte if he could use the table in the meeting room, and it needed to be cleared. Charlotte, Gary said, attempted to deflect the task to Carrie – only that Carrie had to answer the phone did Charlotte go and help him after all. And not long after Phyl and I arrived this morning, Carrie showed Jeff the deposit box, because Charlotte said she had something important to be getting on with and went off somewhere."

"Can you be sure she didn't?" asked D.S. Nasir. "Have something important, that is?"

I gave another little chuckle. "As I discovered only minutes later, the thing of great importance appeared to be no more important than gossiping to a friend on the telephone from inside the toilet cubicle."

"Ah," said the D.S.

"Indeed. If we follow that pattern, it doesn't seem at all farfetched that Charlotte either simply deposited the Insulin into the rubbish bin, or foisted it upon Carrie. However, one can deduce from the accounts given that Charlotte did not return to a position behind the desk after she was seen in the non-fiction sections by Gary, April, Isobel, and Harry. And

I think you will find that the waste bin *is* behind the desk. I expect even our friend P.C. Finbury would be able to ascertain that little detail, but as any time I have heard anyone ask where they can put rubbish, Carrie has said, I'll take it and drop it in the bin, so I expect I am quite correct about it, don't you think?"

"Just a moment, Sally." There was a shuffle and a scrape and a scuffle of chair on carpet and the harrumphing that tends to go with a person getting up from an uncomfortable seat. The shadowy blur that was the D.S. moved towards the desk, allowing the full rectangular brightness of the window to lighten the table at which I remained.

A moment later, she was back. "There are two bins," she said, matter-of-factly. "One appears to be for paper and is quite full. The other has a couple of crisp packets and the like. I can't see a bin anywhere in this section, although I wouldn't be surprised if there is one in each meeting room. But what makes you think Charlotte or Carrie put it in the bin? If one of them put it in the bin, it could hardly have been used to kill Charlotte a few minutes later."

I had to explain that she was getting a bit ahead of herself, and that my suggestion was not that it had actually been deposited into the waste receptacle at that moment, although it did seem likely it had, in fact, been thrown away sometime later. "After it had been used to inject its contents into poor Charlotte. After it was found for the *second* time this morning."

"Ah." D.S. Nasir pulled out the chair, moved across the brighter grey oblong of light, and sat once more.

"It is perfectly logical to suppose April handed the pen to Charlotte, at which time Charlotte simply set it upon the desk or handed it to Carrie. I imagined Charlotte then continued with whatever she was doing, which we now know was stacking the pile of books Isobel had given her. We can agree she had not finished stacking the books, as she clearly had some of them about her person when she was attacked, hence the *Victorian Needlecraft* and *Garden Design* Kimberley retrieved from the floor a short time ago. Carrie, more observant or attentive than Charlotte, realised immediately what it was that Charlotte had just given her, and immediately saw an opportunity. One might very well imagine that she popped the Insulin pen into her pocket. If questioned, she would most likely protest she was keeping it safe until its owner could be determined. Perhaps that was, initially, her intention and it was only once she had it safely about her person that the ideas came to her."

"Hmm. Burning a hole in her pocket, you mean?" D.S. Nasir sounded terribly thoughtful and I could just make out a sound not unlike that made by a gently dripping tap. I wondered if she might be tapping a finger against her lips in the way some of my most studious pupils might have done when attempting to analyse a particularly difficult piece of poetry or whatnot.

"Exactly. You see, in a remarkably short space of time, Gary had been seen with Charlotte; Harry had been observed cornering her, and Isobel had been sent to her to deliver an armful of books. All three, as we now know, had some kind of motive for causing harm to Charlotte: Isobel wanted to get her out of the way to free the path to Harry's affections. Gary harboured a grudge following Charlotte's interference with his marriage. Harry, meanwhile, was driven to terrible behaviour by the passions of unrequited love. Three people, each seen in her presence, each with a possible reason to do her harm."

"Mm. And Carrie, you think, knew all that?"

"Yes. One must allow that Carrie may not have *intended* anything. She may have simply slipped the insulin in her pocket and gone to Charlotte for another reason. Nonetheless, upon finding her in a secluded spot, with no one watching, I am quite certain that she plunged the insulin into her, rolled the pen back under the shelf, and called out as if she had just found her there."

"Quite the risk."

"The only person, aside from Charlotte, who knew the insulin had already been picked off the floor was April, and I feel quite certain Carrie was quite unaware of that fact. I imagine Charlotte simply passed the pen to Carrie, with some abrupt comment such as 'Found it on the floor,' if she bothered to say anything at all and didn't merely drop it onto the counter for Carrie to attend to. We know there was no love lost between them, and they were not the type to stand around chatting to one another. Carrie, most likely, was unaware that April had already found the pen, and that, I would think, was the flaw in Carrie's plan."

"I imagine the police would have uncovered something to point towards her, given time." The D.S. kept her voice level and dry, but I would not be at all surprised if there hadn't been a little smile tugging at her mouth. One can hear a smile in another's voice, don't you agree?

"If Carrie presumed Charlotte herself had found it," I said, "and thus assumed no one but Charlotte would know it had already been handed in, she could simply toss it back under the shelves, in the approximate location of where she knew Charlotte to have found it. And that, of course, is where Kimberly spotted it, after it had been used to kill poor Charlotte."

"Mm," D.S. Nasir agreed. "And quite the stroke of luck on Carrie's part that the pen belonged to Isobel. One of the last people seen with Charlotte."

"Indeed. And a second stroke of luck that the first people to come to Carrie's assistance when she pretended to discover Charlotte lying on the floor were the other two people most likely to have wished her ill. All she had to do, at that point, was maintain her usual professional demeanour and let the others accuse each other, which was remarkably easy, as she had already established motives or opportunity for each one."

"Goodness, Sally, you do seem to have it all sewn up, don't you."

"I have no doubt there will be a handful of loose ends for you to deal with. You will need to confirm everything I have said, of course, as I cannot be entirely certain of the angles of things and whether someone may have seen something to negate some of my notions. Nonetheless, I think you will agree there are certain deductions I have offered from which you may begin."

From the far side of the counter, there came a great pounding on the door, giving me quite the fright. I had quite forgotten Finbury had left the library, what with all the excitement of solving the puzzle with the Detective Sergeant whilst he had been absent.

"I suppose we should let him back in." D.S. Nasir said it so quietly one might have imagined she was speaking her thoughts aloud. I gave a little chuckle to let her know I agreed with the sentiment, and up she got again. "Come along Sally, take my arm." She helped me to my feet and tucked my hand into the crook of her arm. "I'll pop you back to your friends and then I'll let him know he can put some handcuffs on Carrie and whisk her off to the station. Perhaps I'll even let him use the lights and the siren."

Chapter Twenty

With one hand tucked through the D.S.'s arm, and the other on Amity's harness, the D.S. and Amity guided me safely across the laminate and away from the impatient pounding on the door. We had not taken a great many steps when a worrying thought occurred to me. I halted in my steps with such abruptness that I gave the poor D.S.'s arm quite the jerk. "Goodness!"

"What is it, Sally?"

I told her that I had just realised Little Wittering would be left without a librarian for the immediate future. "Our esteemed councillors may take it upon themselves to use these unfortunate circumstances to make some of those dreaded cuts one keeps hearing about." I wriggled my hand free and gave her arm a little pat. "But don't you worry about that now. I am sure you have quite enough to be dealing with."

The pounding came again, which rather proved my point. I told her she had better go and attend to her colleague, as I was sure we were terribly near to other meeting room and Amity could guide me perfectly well.

She didn't seem entirely sure about letting me go off alone, so I called out, "Hellooo, would one of you mind assisting me back to my seat so D.S. Nasir can go and deal with the constable?"

Someone jumped up terribly quickly, as a dark shadow loomed towards us, accompanied by first the padding of footsteps on the carpet for one or two paces and then the clop of shoes on laminate. I wasn't at all surprised when it turned out to be Kimberly. She had been seated closest to the action for most of the morning and I couldn't see any reason why she might have chosen to sit elsewhere for the *denouement*, as it were.

"Kimberly will take me from here, won't you dear? And I'll have a word with Phyllis and see if she mightn't be able to sort something out for the library, as she is still terribly sharp and capable. She only took her retirement because Frederick nagged about it. Of course, they may simply decide we could have Dafydd back again, with his lovely Welsh accent and friendly manner, and that would be a bit of a silver lining to the whole affair."

The Detective Sergeant said she really didn't think she could help with that problem, but she would go and let P.C. Finbury in, and then pop back into the meeting room and have a word with Carrie. She tucked my arm quite neatly into Kimberly's arm, and off she went to put a stop to the infuriating little gimlet's impatient pounding on the door before he had the whole thing down.

Kimberley got me into the meeting room, and the D.S. got Finbury back into the library. All at once, the fired-up tones of his loudmouth opinions wafted into earshot. Of course, D.S. Nasir is terribly efficient and discreet about things so it would have been almost impossible to hear what she might have been saying to Finbury unless she intended it to be overheard. You won't be at all surprised to learn that we could deduce entirely the content of the conversation. It took a few minutes for her to cover the gist of the matter, but it wasn't terribly long before Finbury all but squealed with delight, so I supposed she had said about the siren-and-lights idea.

Not very long after that, she came and took Carrie off to chat about what had happened to poor Charlotte.

I supposed Carrie must have admitted to it all by then, although we could only make out the odd snippets. At first, she sounded terribly contrite about it, but then she became quite belligerent, and said Charlotte had deserved all she'd got, so I found it terribly difficult to muster any sympathy for her in the end.

After a while the D.S. said quite clearly, "I don't suppose we need to put the cuffs on you, but I must caution you." With that, she immediately recited the caution, and it was exactly as they do it on the television, so that was rather exciting if one overlooked the fact that a respected librarian was being carted away in a police car.

D.S. Nasir did as she had said, which was of little surprise as she is exactly the kind of person who keeps her word, so Finbury got to accompany Carrie in the police car and the D.S. came back in to us, and sure enough, just as the doors swooshed closed, there was the squeal of the siren.

"Has he put on the lights?" I asked, and everyone said yes, in quite the mix of excitement and sorrow, so that was that.

Detective Sergeant Nasir said she hadn't quite finished with us, which just goes to show how thorough she is about loose ends and whatnots. As she took her place amongst us in the meeting room, I was reassured once again that she is a perfectly suitable person to hold such a superior position in the police force. She asked a few final questions and said she was sorry we'd all had such an arduous morning, then she thanked us for our time and patience. "You are all free to leave."

Most of us said it had been no trouble, and I suspect some of us had found it quite thrilling, but of course one mustn't overlook the fact that a librarian was dead, which rather took the edge of the excitement.

"Sally," D.S. Nasir said quietly, laying gentle fingers on my arm, "you have been very helpful. It was quite the pleasure to meet again. Perhaps," she added, "we will meet one another in more pleasant circumstances, one day."

I said I hoped as much, but I was happy to have been of some assistance and perhaps there was benefit in reading those old Agatha Christie books. I decided there and then to suggest we do another one for our next read, just in case it might have any useful hints for the future, and everyone had a bit of a chuckle about that.

"How about a nice romance?" Ashwini said. "See if we can find a happy ending for our poor Bel. She's had quite the shock, I should think."

"Not with Harry," Joan muttered from the end of the table.

"No," agreed the D.S. "I dare say we might have a bit of a word with him, about unwarranted attention and stalking, once we have Carrie sorted out." She got herself up and took herself off to complete the paperwork or interrogate Carrie or whatever it might be one does once one has arrested someone, and we all fell silent for about thirty seconds and then everyone started up at once to talk about it all.

"There is just one thing that remains a mystery," I said. "Isobel, how *did* you know it was a woman who had come to harm?"

"What do you mean?"

"When we first realised someone was in trouble, you said *she* probably had a fit. How did you know it was a *she*?"

"I don't know. I didn't. I suppose I just presumed, what with all of us being female, and there not being many men in the library?" Her voice rose into a question, indicating that she didn't sound at all convinced of her own protestations.

I turned my face towards her voice and waited.

"And," she said very quietly, "I had just seen Harry and Charlotte fighting, and even though I thought they had stopped, I guess I was afraid he'd gone back and done something to her. I'm very glad he hadn't."

Of course, we all agreed about that, and when the hubbub died down, some of our little group left quite quickly, but as I'm sure you can quite imagine, with all the excitement and the chatter, it took another thirty minutes or thereabouts before the rest of us got ourselves ready to leave. There was quite the kerfuffle as to what to do about the library now both the librarians had been removed from the premises. After my little chat about that with D.S. Nasir, she had instructed Finbury to telephone the council and make a report, but by the time they'd bundled Carrie into one of the police cars, no one had arrived.

Phyllis had kicked up quite the fuss when the D.S. said we could be on our way, protesting that we couldn't possibly leave the building unsecured. Some of the others agreed with her, although others, such as poor Isobel, made a dash for freedom just as soon as the D.S. said we were free to leave. I can't say I blamed her at all as it must have been quite the shock to have been accused of murdering a librarian, however short-lived the accusation might have been. Josephine had said perhaps Mary wouldn't mind going with her, to make sure she got to the chemist or wherever she might be able to get a new dose of insulin, since Finbury had got her quite the wrong thing. After a little discussion about it, Ashwini said she'd pop her over to the surgery and make sure Dr Patil got her sorted out, so she'd gone with them too, and that was quite the relief, I'm sure you agree.

Gary, as I have mentioned, is terribly practical, so he hung around for a little while to see what he could do to help with anything. Phyllis is not the kind of person to miss a trick, so she soon put Gary to good use following her instructions to keep the library ticking over until the woman from the council eventually turned up. I must say that the council woman was not at all satisfactory, as all she did was fix a 'Closed due to an emergency' notice to the door with half a roll of Sellotape, and turn us all out onto the street with no idea as to whether we would be able to meet for our book club on the following Tuesday or not.

"That nice Detective Sergeant said we should meet at the park, while the weather is good," I said, as we stood in front of the library and debated what to do for the best.

Barbara gave a most hearty kind of snort and said that would put an end to the summer before it had begun, and we had quite the chuckle about that and I said I expected she was right and I'd said very much the same myself.

In the end, we agreed that those of us left would take ourselves down to the hotel, and see if they might have a room we could make use of as a temporary measure. Josephine said it might soften them up if we had lunch while we were at it, and Joan said if we didn't mind going along at the pace of a somnolent snail, she'd enjoy a nice lunch as it had been donkey's years since she'd been out for lunch in the hotel. April, who I'd quite forgotten was still there, said, "Oh, how sweet, there's that funny little phrase about donkeys again," so of course we said we'd make her an honorary member for the rest of the day if she'd like to join us. Then of course Gary said he'd come too, if men were allowed, to which Harry immediately retorted, "Not me, I'm off." He still sounded most tearful, so I suspect it was beginning to sink in that Charlotte was gone. Barbara had a moment of rare seriousness, and said perhaps if he went along to the hospital and explained that he was her boyfriend, they might let him pop in to wherever it was they'd taken her so her so he could say his goodbyes. Phyl agreed at once, as it was terribly common in Ireland to pay one's respects and everyone in Ireland was terribly used to seeing the deceased and it might be a very good idea and help him come to terms with it.

No one uttered a word about the fact that Charlotte had not, in fact, thought Harry *was* her boyfriend anymore, which I must say was terribly kind and sympathetic of everyone.

The woman from the council must have come out behind us, because there was the swooshing of the door and the clunk of a key turning in a lock, and then the sound of the outer door swooshing closed and another click of a lock. It sounded terribly final and I did have a little worry that the library might not recover, but Phyl squeezed my arm and said, "Come on Sally, let's not worry about it anymore today," and tucked my hand into the crook of my elbow. "Come on Amity, let's get our Sal up to the hotel and have ourselves a good lunch and perhaps we've earned a little tipple after all the excitement."

Barbara said that was a jolly good idea, so despite the sad circumstances, we were quite a cheerful group as we set off down the road. Gary walked along beside Joan to help her with the pavement, and behind them, Phyl and Amity came either side of me. Ahead of us Barbara and Josephine chatted away nineteen-to-the-dozen, although I couldn't tell you what they were talking about, and you never know with Barbara so it really could have been anything. Bringing up the rear came Kimberly and April, with Kimberly telling April she didn't know how she'd managed to end up in Little Wittering on such a day, as usually, it was a very sleepy little town where nothing very exciting ever happens. Phyl and I and Josephine all agreed whole-heartedly with that sentiment, although Barbara gave one of her little tuts and said nothing ever surprised her, to tell the truth, and then we were at the Hotel, and up we went into the lounge. However, once we'd got ourselves in, we quickly agreed we'd just about missed lunch but could show April a perfectly delectable afternoon tea in the lounge.

Of course, that is exactly what we did, and after she'd had quite the share of the scones and jam, April agreed that it was perfectly pleasant in Little Wittering after all. "Isn't it exactly how I'd imagined a small English town to be!" she said, in a terribly satisfied kind of way, which just goes to show how quickly one can get over a shock, don't you agree?

We sat there chattering until it was awfully late into the afternoon, and Dennis got me on the telephone and said was he going to have to get his own tea, and I'd never guess what excitement there'd been in town that morning. I had a little chuckle and said, no, I don't suppose I would, but if he'd like to come along and collect me and Phyl, we'd tell him all about it on the way home.

Acknowledgements

As ever, my biggest thanks are to you, my readers. I can't begin to describe the thrill of knowing people read the books I write. Thank you, too, for your patience as I took my sweet time to get this book written. Some of you will know I had some challenges over the past eighteen months, and even as I put the finishing touches of this book together, I am still recovering after an accident in which I injured my leg. I'm as glad to have finally got the book finished as I hope you are!

I also, as always, thank my husband for his ongoing support. I really couldn't do this without him.

Thank you as always to Shayne, my amazing cover-designer-become-friend. She can be found at www.wickedgoodbookcovers.com

Thank you to Eilidh, who has brought four more characters to life with her wonderful portraits of Carrie, Gary, Bel, and Harry. More of Eilidh's art can be found at www.instagram.com/aileemarie_art

Thank you to my wonderful audio narrator Helen Lloyd, who has once again done a brilliant job of giving voice to Sally Smith for the audio edition of this book.

The following is a repeat of the information I wrote in the back of the first Mrs Smith's Suspects book, *Claude, Gord, Alice, and Maud*. I've added it again in case this is your first foray into Mrs Smith's world, and you are wondering what gives me the authority to write from a blind character's point of view.

I hope you are enjoying getting to know Mrs Sally Smith as much as I am. Like Sally Smith, my paternal grandmother became blind in adulthood, due to diabetic glaucoma, not long before I was born. I only have a handful of memories of her, as she died when I was very young, but she brushed my hair more gently than anyone (and I had very tangly hair). I would sit in her dim basement kitchen, and she would gently, so gently, unknot my tangles with her fingers and a red Mason Pearson hairbrush. I also have a vivid snapshot memory of walking along a road with her and her guide dog, Amber, although I have no idea where we had been or where we were going.

Amber lived on for several years after Grandma died, with first my grandfather and then my aunt, and I remember her with far more clarity than I remember either of my grandparents. Writing Mrs Smith has reminded me of them all, and has had me poring over pictures of the two grandparents I hardly had time to know, and quizzing my dad and my aunt on long-forgotten memories of their mother. I've felt a sadness over not knowing her that I hadn't really considered before, but also an incredible pleasure in writing this book, as, by putting myself in my grandma's shoes as I navigate Mrs Smith's world, I feel I've got to know my grandma better.

About the Author

For up-to-date news and exclusive content including maps, images, and extra stories about the characters in Jinny's cozy mystery series, please sign up for Jinny's newsletter by popping over to her website and choosing one of the free short stories listed there:

www.jinnyalexander.com

Say hello at facebook.com/JinnyAlexanderAuthor

If you enjoyed the book, please take a moment to leave a review on Amazon and Goodreads. Thank you.

Jinny was first published in Horse and Pony magazine at the age of ten. She's striving to achieve equal accolades now she's (allegedly) a grown-up. Jinny has been placed or listed in writing competitions including the prestigious Bath Flash Fiction Award and Flash500. She has been published in MsLexia Magazine and Writing Magazine, among other publishing credits. Jinny has recently completed an MA in Creative Writing with the University of Hull, for which she was awarded a Distinction.

Jinny is the author of the Jess O'Malley Irish Village Mystery Series, the Mrs Smith's Suspects cosy mystery series, and a handful of standalone novels.

Jinny also teaches English as a foreign language to people all over the world and finds her students a constant source of inspiration for both life and stories. Her home, for now, is in rural Ireland, which she shares with her husband and far too many animals. Her two children have grown and flown, but return across the Irish Sea when they can.

Also by Jinny Alexander

The Jess O'Malley Irish Village Mystery Series

Jinny is currently working on more sequels to both series. She has also written a non-fiction diary of her work as an online teacher of English as a second language, *Don't Squeeze the Turtle*, released in summer 2025.

Jinny also has stories and flash fiction in anthologies and magazines. A more comprehensive list can be found on her website at www.jinnyalexander.com

Dear Isobel (March 2022, Creative James Media) is currently out of print following Jinny's reversion of rights.

Praise for *A Diet of Death*

This is a light-hearted cosy that will delight fans of
M C Beaton's Agatha Raisin. […] Highly
recommend it to those looking for a frothy,
enjoyable read that is low on violence and high on
feel-good entertainment!

MAIRI CHONG,
The Dr. Cathy Moreland Mysteries

Well-written and intriguing, this mystery
revolving around members of a weight-loss
group is one that will keep you turning the
pages until the very end.

KELLY YOUNG,
The Travel Writer Cozy Mystery Series

A classic British style whodunnit.
With an engaging and believable heroine - Jess O'Malley - and
set in rural Ireland, this is a fun mystery with lots of heart.
An enjoyable read leading to a satisfying solution, already
looking forward to the next book.

GERALDINE MOORKENS BYRNE
The Caroline Jordan Mystery series and *On
the Fiddle! The Music Shop Mysteries*

The whole book was a warm, comforting read for
anyone who loves mysteries. Highly suggested for
fans of *The Thursday Murder Club.*

ALISON WEATHERBY,
The Secrets Act

Jinny Alexander's outstanding cosy mystery
A Diet Of Death is a real treat.
(And not the kind with calories!)

J. IVANEL JOHNSON,
The JUST (e)STATE Cozy Mysteries

This tale is a homage to those much loved
classic detective authors, and is perfect for
escaping the worries and stresses of the world.

LOUISE MORRISH,
Operation Moonlight

Jinny Alexander embeds her murder mystery with the satisfying
atmosphere of rural Ireland. […] Cozy mystery readers who enjoy stories
of friendships and murder possibilities will find *A Diet of Death* unusually
strong in its atmosphere, which does equal justice to both the murder
mystery component and the entwined lives of a small village […]

MIDWEST BOOK REVIEW